The Last Resort Library

The
Last Resort
Library

written by

Irving Finkel

Irving Finkel

and illustrated by

Jenny Kallin

Jenny Kallin

Kennedy & Boyd
an imprint of
Zeticula
57 St Vincent Crescent
Glasgow
G3 8NQ
Scotland

http://www.kennedyandboyd.co.uk
admin@kennedyandboyd.co.uk

Text Copyright © Irving Finkel 2007
Illustrations Copyright © Jenny Kallin 2007

ISBN-13 978 1 904999 41 6
ISBN-10   1 904999 41 7

For
Joanna
&
Ivor

Prologue

"The library is situated,"

said the short entry in the *Guide to British Libraries* A-L,

> "in pleasant rolling countryside
> not too far from Hereford, and is
> perhaps most readily accessible
> by private motor vehicle."

This statement was quite accurate. Inaccessibility had always been one of the Library's most prized qualities.

> "The Last Resort Library was
> founded in 1962, and is a forward-
> looking institution with very
> much its own sense of mission,"

it continued.

The truth was that the *Guide* compiler had never heard of the Library himself, but someone had mentioned it to him right at the last minute, and he was improvising while correcting proofs.

> "Researchers should be aware that,
> despite the size of the Library's
> holdings, there is no published
> catalogue of any kind."

That's what he had been told, and it seemed only sensible to make a formal note of it.

🖛 1 🖚

The Last Resort Library was always at its worst in the rain. The roof leaked enthusiastically in most of the buildings, despite a parade of long-suffering practitioners who struggled with deficiencies and short-cuts inherited from the original workmen. Rain meant having to run around with a tray of vessels, and on really bad days there would be an orchestration of varied pings as the tin buckets and empty coffee-jars fought to resist the invader.

It was raining now, hard against the glass, as the Porter gazed out absently through his steamy kitchen window, embedded in the warmth of his cottage. The radio was on softly, and he yawned, awkwardly extracting his wife's toast before it carbonised.

The outer bell jangled insistently.

'Oh, Lord, not again. They've been already this morning, haven't they, Millie? Or was that yesterday?'

Millie sighed sympathetically, spreading marmalade.

'No, it was half an hour ago. Perhaps they found another box. Or maybe it's a wandering minstrel, or a charismatic preacher. Someone about the drains, even. Our life is replete with the novel.'

Her husband snorted.

'Our life is over-replete with novels. I do hope it isn't Dan with a new donation. The Chief won't like it. Not on a Friday. Put the kettle back on, Millie. I'll go and see. Where did I put the damn keys…?'

He disappeared out into the passage, and trudged out up to their front gate.

'Yes,' said the Porter. 'Look, who is it? The world is a blur in the middle of breakfast.'

'Cool down, Steve,' said the driver. 'It's only me again, but wearing my Special Delivery hat. I was going to leave it till

Monday, but this one's got *Special* stamped all over it. I'll need a hand, I'm afraid. Looks like another *Complete Works*.'

'Jeez. What a week. Living or dead?'

'Oh, firmly dead, I hope. Anything more would be indecent. You might bring the trolley, Steve. Perhaps we can manage it in one trip.'

The Porter hesitated.

'What initial is it?'

'Hold on, they're all in sacks. The labels say ...a Mrs ... *Wilberforce* from Southampton. Yep, it's a "W" all right. Weren't you proposing a little flutter this time? I think that's one beer you owe me, Stevie boy ...'

The Porter stepped onto the gravel, tugging the trolley behind him.

'Don't jump to conclusions, Dan. Could be, say, the dispatcher is a married daughter. Might even be a false name altogether, if it's really grim stuff. I tell you, man, we've got things here you wouldn't believe. I have to be really careful these days what I let Millie unpack.'

'I know. It's life in the raw out here. A man can hardly eat his breakfast in peace for gratuitous deliveries of smut.'

'Smut, schmut. Smut's by no means the worst of it. Better a happy-go-lucky fellow like yourself should remain in ignorance, take my word.'

'You're probably right. I've always been far too happy-go-lucky, and ... sensitive. You're a brave man, Steve, shielding us all from endless pornography.'

The heavy parcels were manoeuvred onto the trolley.

'O.K. That's the lot. I'll leave you in peace.'

'You must come in for a nibble one of these days, Daniel. Week before Christmas, say?'

'In there? All that pernicious stuff lying about would ruin my appetite, even for Millie's sausages.'

'There's none of it in our flat, don't you worry. We only have Real Books here.'

'Well, that's the lot for this week. It really never ends, does it?'

'One of these days we may have to think about extending again, the Principal was saying recently. We are getting better known all the time and our authors are, as you might say, legion.'

'Yep.'

The Porter closed the great front door, and parked the laden trolley in the passage. He hung up his coat, muttering under his breath.

'Wonder what we've got here? So-called Fact or so-called Fiction? Loads of "Literature" or piles of "Poetry"?'

'Oh, there you are dear. Wondered what happened to you. Big delivery?'

'Biggish for a goodish while, Mill. Several sacks. I'll leave it here until we've finished, then I'll have to report it upstairs.'

'Shall I start on the unstitching?'

'No, we'll do it together as we always do.'

Dr Patience shifted irritably in his Principal Librarian's chair. His door was shut and he was supposed to be hard at work on the *Booklet*. Several members of his staff had mentioned that it would be useful to have some kind of manifesto for the Last Resort Library. In the outside world his Librarians could find themselves on the wrong side of awkward questions, and a considered statement from the top of what the Library was there for would be really useful. In addition, they were often asked how it had come into existence, and how it managed to hold on in a competitive and hard-bitten world. Such a document would have real benefits, he knew, but the thing wasn't exactly writing itself. His first thought had been to dash off a single sheet of A4 with a short-attention-span "mission statement," but lately he had come to think that an illustrated booklet would be more in order. Rosemary Ogilvie, his trusted Secretary and indispensable right hand, was looking out photographs and memorabilia from Archives to provide the illustrations. Meanwhile he was pursuing the Registrar, Hugo de Butler, for a rough estimate of their holdings to date. 'Just an outline summary,' he had suggested, but Hugo had frowned grievously, a finely-tuned instinct warning him at once just how much effort would be involved in providing suitable facts.

Dr Patience was trying this morning to get to grips with the *Introduction*. The thing was to find a snappy and interesting style to grab the reader from the outset. Light, that meant, but authoritative. He still had no idea at all how to *begin* the thing. He opened the file and started reading over some of his earlier paragraphs, fountain pen at the ready.

The timing of that purchase was fortuitous. For years the great Sir Bulward Bulward's career had lurched unpredictably between opulence and ruin, but just at

that period he was enjoying a run of uninterrupted affluence. Tipped at Oxford as a highly-promising new novelist, his first slim and confessional volume had been drastically over-blown by the media, and he came to learn at first hand the fickle nature of Literature as a career. There were episodes concerning racehorses and property speculation, and murmurs of darker things, but in the end manipulations at the lower end of the magazine trade netted him a huge and well-publicised fortune. Would-be writers now flocked to him with hard-luck stories, and requests for assistance or patronage persecuted him in an endless stream.

Too conversational? Perhaps. But Bulward had certainly enjoyed a complex career, not to mention a little notoriety now and again, and some flavour of the man needed to come across. He would probably merit, in due course, a full biography. But a more conventional start to the *Introduction* was necessary.

An unfamiliar name to most, the Last Resort Library has been going quietly about its business since 1963, twenty-three years ago at the time of writing. That was the year in which the Founder, Sir Bulward Bulward, discovered the ideal spot of land - with its sprawling, ramshackle farmhouse – that today forms the nucleus of his revolutionary and visionary Library.

Why stress their obscurity? Pedestrian, too, on re-reading. He drew a line through it. He would try again later, or maybe get Rosemary to think of something. He read on a bit.

The stimulus for the foundation of the Library had been the messy suicide of an intimate college friend whom he had always known to be a far better writer than himself, leaving an entire life's work unpublished and unwanted. Strolling supportively beside the undernourished widow at the funeral, the Founder offered impulsively to purchase the entire output,

*thinking that with all his contacts he must be able to
get at least something into print on her behalf. That
afternoon, drinking on expansively in the company of
peers less prosperous and well-known than himself, the
idea of posthumous rescue publication seemed to him
refreshing, and, driving back erratically to London
that evening, he had even permitted himself a passing
fantasy about translation possibilities and film rights.*

*Sir Bulward's notes record how taken aback he was
when his driver staggered in with the manuscript
cartons a week later, and thoroughly appalled at the
unanticipated pile of correspondence that accompanied
them. Twenty years of fruitless endeavour had generated
a quantity of offensive rejection letters that made up
more than a book in itself. The correspondence was
neatly punched and filed in strict chronological order.
The whole consignment thus represented the sum of one
individual's thwarted creative life, and the Founder,
seated on the floor awash in paper, had been struck into
silence by its implications.*

*The major vision, the Last Resort Library, had come
upon him shortly thereafter in a burst of illumination,
and had taken several days to crystallize into a
definable plan. He had collected a mistress, jumped into
a Bentley, and driven out of London on the hunt for a
suitable property.*

And here we are, children, he thought, here we are.

*The day that the purchase was effected, his fatigued
but obedient lawyers were instructed to institute
an architectural competition to develop a material
home for the fruits of the articulated conception. A
philanthropist who had grown to manhood in some of
England's most elegant libraries naturally required a
fine Reading Room of his own, and storage would be*

needed to accommodate collections whose dimensions Sir Bulward, with a blitheness that later seemed incredible, thought he anticipated correctly.

'Indeed,' said Dr Patience out loud, 'you can say that again, sunshine.'

For some reason only a mishmash of architects seemed to have submitted designs for the library complex competition. On top of that, one of the judging panel died in a road accident, and another, according to the second Principal Librarian, completely lost his detachment after being trapped for two days in an elevator in one of his own tower blocks. As it turned out, however, they were fortunate in their winner, who proved able to translate Sir Bulward's vaguely-sketched "look, like *this*," back-of-an-envelope plans into reality and elegance.

The library grew as if by magic. The farmhouse was converted into Sir Bulward's coveted high-ceilinged and roughly circular Reading Room. Other meandering sections were built on to act as the librarians' studies, and, of course, to provide storage. The largest of the adjacent barns, now mostly invisible, formed the kernel of the Conference Centre, created in the hope that the Library would come to be a pivotal meeting place for scholars of what the Founder liked to call the "unsung song." Sir Bulward himself took up at least partial residence in the imported Tower House, gathering around him a handful of disillusioned or inexpensive librarians, and the Library declared itself open for business.

Handsome enough on the inside, the home of the Last Resort Library was mostly outwardly unappealing. It had improved substantially since the pioneer days, what with the maturing trees, the grey of the once intimidating outer fences now subdued by a veneer of moss and wind-blown leaves, but such visitors as came upon it by chance divined at once that there was something of the secret research-station about the place, and usually drove on. Dr Patience himself had been overheard at conferences to praise the buildings for their *austerity*, but this doubtful quality did little to compensate for the binocular, prison-like greyness of the outer library structures.

(The next pages were in manuscript. With untidy corrections. He would have to get it all typed up.)

> *The dead friend's output was, inevitably, the first and most revered item in the Library's holdings, housed on two shelves of its own set off with a small engraved brass plaque.*
> *The Last Resort Library never troubled to publicise itself in a conventional way. Its self-declared role,* to house and rescue for Posterity manuscripts that no-one at all ever wanted to publish, *meant that they were guaranteed widespread and enduring support. There would always be writers who qualified, and the Last Resort Library began almost from its inception to grow with the alacrity and the abandon of the national copyright libraries.*

Dr Patience looked up, and loosened his tie thoughtfully. Working side by side with the Founder almost from those first weeks had been a sardonic but clear-thinking professional librarian who had recently been passed over for major promotion in the university library in which he had selflessly laboured for more than thirty years. He should be mentioned somewhere: they were all still grateful to him. What was his damn name? Woodrow. That was it.

> *From the very beginning the Library was run with a librarian's principles and rigour; volumes were accessed, numbered and stored in recognised categories, and indeed the whole working operation was always able to stand critical comparison with that of many better-known and more conventional institutions.*

It was Librarian Woodrow, of course, who sharpened and stiffened up the Founder's all-embracing and perhaps romantic approach. Certain fundamental laws were established while day-to-day procedures ensured that material which did not tally one hundred percent with the Library's policy could never enter the collection. The policy in question found written expression in the latter months of the first year under the title *Policy Document 1*. That could be reprinted in the *Booklet*, maybe?

What else? Bloody visitors. Something careful about that. Science and the labs, of course. Sketch something out; get the others to write it up.

> *Visitors, at least from the time that the Visitors' Book had been introduced under the second Principal Librarian, were never that numerous, and there had been little excuse to extend the number of readers' desks, or upgrade the rather primitive facilities in the Lecture Theatre. The tumbling and relentless waterfall of acquisitions produced conflicting responses in the staff. The collection and safe-keeping of their special charges was, after all, their raison d'être, but the buildings in time grew full to overflowing, and a hodge-podge of subsidiary outgrowths sprang up around the original complex to house specific collections. It was less than perfect, and in some spots far less.*

Then, he thought, there had been the laboratory, built on in the late sixties with its crucial dual role of Conservation and Research. The white-coats were always clamouring for more money, some of the staff being conscious through glossy brochures handed out at conferences of seductive new apparatus on the market that would come in very handy, which often made them envious and unsettled when they returned to work. He would have to get Dr Scranton to write up something about their activities, too. And they were still needing to recruit another scientist, now he thought about it.

> *And then, one afternoon about eight years later, the Founder had been found dead in the grounds, watched*

over in the rain by his two matching poodles. The papers had a field day about the "paper tiger," and claimants real and imaginary pressed round the very hearse, but somehow Sir Bulward's careful arrangements for his Last Resort Library stood fast. Its future was pronounced secure in the light of certain judicious investments and remarkable endowments, and the Founder's successors have never had to worry about the survival of the institution, or the salaries of its growing permanent staff.

That was true. Remarkable and true. But he wouldn't go into details, perhaps... It was clear that the staff, paralysed without their charismatic leader, had been distraught to a man. Records went awry at that time, for sure. Not that that concerned the outside world either. But, thinking it over, something more extensive than this should definitely be written about Sir Bulward. A man of mixed and conflicting parts. He would need to put in something here about his own predecessor, and something about himself in the same vein, probably. He idled with an experimental paragraph or two...

Dr Dr Cloudesly Montague Patience [yes, folks, that's two PhD's: you don't often see that, eh?], *the third Principal Librarian to occupy this grand oak-lined study, has now been in post for about four years. He had wisely been snatched up with unanimous agreement by the Library's three Trustees as possessing in abundance all the necessary but rare qualities needed to keep their library running peacefully in the shadows on its timeless, visionary course. And by Jove it had been a good appointment. After a damned impressive University career characterised by vast creativity and influential networking, Dr Patience had also put in time on the "other side," both in a major public library, and in a rather arcane scholarly library that seldom witnessed more than a dozen reader visits per year.*

Montague Patience (he continued, his thoughts flowing easily) *thus brought with him the idea, perhaps traditional among many of his profession, that books are better left undisturbed on shelves than suffer exposure to the rude demands of readers; like many, he was always troubled by unsightly gaps in a neat row of spines. Nevertheless, the flame of research that had been kindled by his own long-dead tutor burned on bravely, and he was by no means averse to scholarship among his staff. If anything, he encouraged it. As a result, all of his colleagues were engaged in research of one kind or another on the manuscripts in their care.*

A problem that remained unsolved in the Principal Librarian's mind was whether scholarly papers produced on the basis of the library's highly individual resources should not, morally speaking, remain unpublished themselves. The conundrum was in every way academic, however, in that no one on the staff in living memory was actually known to have brought a piece of literary endeavour of this kind to a state of completion...

'Who is it?'

The knock at his door had been only just noticeable.

'Good morning, Principal,' said the Porter a little obsequiously, his head round the door. 'If I could just have a word, since you're leaving shortly for the weekend...?'

'By all means, Stavros, come in, come in. I'm only writing. What's on your mind?'

'It's just that we had a large delivery this morning, Sir, a quite compendious set of non-publications, and I don't think we've had *clearance* on it.'

'You appal me, Stavros. This sort of slip-up shouldn't be happening. What is the donor name, do you recall?'

'A Mrs *Wilberforce*, apparently, sorrowful survivor of what must have been a seriously unfulfilled writer. It's chock full of leather-bound typescripts. I haven't done anything more than unpack them, in advance of receiving the guarantee.'

'Oh, in that case there's no need to worry. I spoke to Mrs Wilberforce herself on the telephone last week. It's my fault - I ought to have told you. It's textbook, actually. Where *are* my ...? Here we are. The husband produced seventy-six novels, eight plays and one or two other more ambitious literary items, and not one was ever published. She's never read any of them, she said. He wrote them in private in his study over about forty-three years. She has most of the *letters* too. They're included.'

'They're usually the best reading I always think.'

'Oh, I quite agree, Stavros. In fact, I have been considering that we might one day publish a compilation of our choicest refusal letters. One could attempt a typology, even.'

'Including agents?'

'Assuredly. We couldn't possibly omit literary agents. Some of them are more poisonous than the publishers.'

'So we can go ahead and process this consignment then, Principal?'

'Absolutely. I'll pop down on Monday or Tuesday and see if the Duty Librarian has any classification problems. There sometimes is with a donor of such extensive output, but one can usually surmount all difficulties with a touch of deft cross-indexing. Pity about the leather, though. Could you ensure that it's looked at in the Lab.?'

'Wilco, Sir. And thank you. Good weekend, Sir.'

☞ 3 ☜

The Principal Librarian hummed to himself at his desk after lunch, toying with a pile of unopened mail, and testing the end of his paperknife on his thumb. He had had quite enough of writing *Introductions* for one day. He opened the topmost envelope and read the contents – a single typed sheet – out loud to himself:

Dear Sir,

I write to you as a last resort. I have written my novel. It has taken me twenty years and three or more marriages to bring it to perfection. I have sent it to thirty-three publishers and eighteen agents. A philistine conspiracy of obdurate blind rejection has been unanimous and absolute. I have today burned all copies but this my original. I entrust this last copy into your care. One day, in a hundred or a thousand years, someone will read it and know it for the masterpiece it is. The package will reach you by tomorrow. By that time I myself shall no longer be reachable, by post or any means. By noon today, in fact, my struggle will be over. Please take care of my seven hundred and nineteen pages. Each one breathes through my blood. They are all I can bequeath to mankind …

Dr Patience picked up the telephone.

'Hello? Is that the Duty Librarian? Good. Principal here. Look, I've taken receipt of a *by-the-time-you-read-this-I'll-be-dead* letter, with the author's manuscript apparently on its way under separate cover. The author's name is … Wyfield B. Twyfield. Could I ask you to make sure that the letter is filed with the book when it arrives as per usual, and maybe check with the local authorities as per the address that he really has done the job? I am always reluctant to take one of these sacrifices at face value without police confirmation, since it's unbelievably annoying if we've already gone through registration and one of them comes back to life. I think we'll have to wait until it's established one way or the other before we decide on classification.'

The telephone rang just as he lowered the receiver.

'Good morning. Can I help you? This is the Principal Librarian speaking.'

'Oh, hello, Dr Patience. This is the late Mr Wilberforce's relict, Mrs Wilberforce. I just wanted to hear whether the late Mr Wilberforce's volumes have been safely delivered? I have been in a tizzy of nerves about them ever since the lorry left-'

'You can put your mind entirely at ease, Mrs Wilber-'

'... and I could never forgive myself if anything happened to the late Mr Wilberforce's papers. Each one is unique, you see. As I told you when you came to the house, only one copy of each, from the Master's hand, and all bound in pigskin ...'

'*Eurgh* ...'

'I do beg your pardon?'

'Forgive me. Mrs Wilberforce, something caught in my throat. It's a trifle draughty in my office. It's probably the scientifically-monitored air-conditioning.'

'*Garlic* pills is what you need, Wilby always used to say. Not that they helped him in the end, though. Did I tell you that he was in the middle of a final epic poem when the Dreaded Angel came? It was to be called *Requiem*. I'll never understand how he *knew*...'

'That is almost too touching for words, Mrs Wilberforce. I wonder that you can speak of it so calmly.'

'I just couldn't send you that one. It seemed too poignant for a library, somehow. Cold, metallic bookshelves. You don't have central heating there, I suppose, do you? You see, *Requiem* is not bound like the others, of course, because it is unfinished. Like Schubert's Symphony but in words.'

'How you must have *suffered*, Mrs Wilberforce. How

terribly sad. Perhaps, however, in time the day might break when you feel that *Requiem* could come to us to be reunited with its fellow manuscripts. When you're quite ready. Our holdings are not actually centrally heated as such, of course, but rather are treated to the most up-to-date and state-of-the-art conservation-approved minutely-controlled micro-climate possible, which ensures- '

'...maybe one day, Dr Patience, maybe one day ...'

'... that all our volumes are comfortable and happy ...'

'... the time will come ...'

'... so to speak.'

He fell silent for a minute, enduring additional slight squeaks from the ear-piece.

' ... mm... a-ha ... mm ... Yes, yes *indeed* ... well ... goodbye, Mrs Wilberforce ... goodbye.'

He replaced the receiver.

'God, what a job. I need a holiday, starting in fifteen minutes' time.'

There was another knock at the door.

'Come in ... if you absolutely *must*... Ah, it's *you*, Dr Brecknock; now, how are you?'

Dr Louis Brecknock had a fresh PhD in English literature from a northern university. His was the sort of appointment to which most of the staff was opposed, but the Principal had snapped him up as representing a type of scholar that he was going to need on board for his Great Plan. Not a leader, but a useful man. Louis was now about twenty-six, with slightly protruding eyes and a prominent Adam's apple. He dressed in an assortment of tweedy brown clothes that he clearly considered literary but which were all too large for his narrow frame, and possibly also second-hand. The Principal was fond of him, and tried to keep an eye on his progress. According to his present contract, Dr Brecknock had two days a week cataloguing, two days for research, and one day for hoovering, as they were temporarily short on cleaners.

'Good morning, Sir. Just come to administer the sheen. Would you care to leave while the machine is in operation? It is raucous when it warms up, as you know.'

'Perhaps I will. How's the research going? What was your subject, finally?'

'Jolly nice of you to enquire, Sir. *Unprinted Poetry by Unprinted Poets beginning with L: Just Unfortunate or Just Unpublishable?* It's all a bit of a problem. One has to read everything first before beginning to write a word oneself.'

It was just this attitude that so appealed to the Principal. Good, solid research. No cutting corners, or skimping. No snatching at theory on the basis of scattered data like so many so-called scholars nowadays.

'The real trouble is, just when I am making a bit of headway, in comes another lot.'

'Your L is a fertile letter, then?'

'Well I'm sure it wasn't during my probation week. But there was a sudden rush. There was that consignment of folios by Mr A. Aylmer Longfellow, you'll remember.'

'I certainly do. We catalogued it as provisionally the longest known rhyming epic in the English language, in the least gratifying handwriting. *Ter tum ti tum ter tum ti tum* it all went, did it not?'

'Yes, and he specialized in rhymes like "faltering man" with "watering can".'

'So he did. And you sense that you will need to read over the entire oeuvre?'

'I do, really. And there are endless contributions here indexed under A. Lover, Your Lover, Her Lover, His Lover and miscellaneous other Lovers. Many of those will be central to any discussion of the process of rejection.'

'I admire your dedication, Mr Brecknock. You wouldn't consider changing to a less demanding letter, perhaps?'

'Not after all I've done, Dr Patience. I just couldn't. And, anyway, who knows what might come in at any time?'

'True enough. Done into Latin, that could be our professional motto. I'll leave you to your meditations and your device.'

He closed the door firmly as the high-pitched whine started up.

'I must find my Secretary. She hasn't mentioned the timetable.'

The Secretary appeared as if by magic.

'Ah, Miss Ogilvie, do you recall what time my train leaves this afternoon?'

'Four-fifteen, Principal. You will need an hour or more to reach the station comfortably. Shall I look out something suitable for the journey from the Rubbish Pile, or will you be purchasing a Real Book yourself from a commercial outlet on the platform?'

'I think today I might venture on a modest worldly publication. It is as well for one of us to keep an occasional eye on conventional manifestations of literature.'

'Just as long as you don't bring it back here afterwards and leave it lying around like on that previous occasion. You know how it unsettles the cataloguers to come upon such things in this building without warning.'

'Point taken, Miss Ogilvie, point taken. I must make an effort to think more about other people.'

'Don't punish yourself unduly, Principal. Some of our younger colleagues are naturally still fervent.'

'Incidentally, Miss O., I have been meaning to ask you about the Rubbish Pile. I passed it on my way in this morning, and it seemed to me that it might be in danger of toppling. Can we not do something to get it off the premises altogether, into the hands of those who *pulp* for their livelihood?'

'It may come to force of arms, Principal. Rejection by the Final Resort Library seems to be hard to take for some. These things just arrive, marked *For the Library*,'

'Cannot they just understand that our responsibility is for genuine and established *failures*, preferably backed up by good-quality derisory paperwork? We are not a repository for inscribed paper at large or unwanted paperbacks.'

'Leave it with me, Principal. They will all be gone by Monday. Meanwhile, you won't forget that we have an important Staff Meeting on Monday *morning* after your return?'

'Oh God, do we really?'

'We do, Dr Patience. Remember that you decided they were a good idea, to "keep everybody informed and feeling important," you said.'

'Did I really? Madness, Miss Ogilvie, madness ...'

☞ 4 ☜

The Staff Meeting was about to begin. People came in noisily, carrying awkward coffees and jostling for seats. The full complement consisted of about sixteen or seventeen staff members, and Dr Sorensen, the Deputy Principal Librarian who had been hoping that he might get to chair the meeting, regretfully spotted Dr Patience hovering in the doorway.

'Ah, Principal. Welcome back. How was your week-end in the outside world?'

'My host thought I should experiment with some "fresh air." Overrated in my view. Mind you, Sigurd,' he continued, lowering his voice, 'we had good talks. His second wife showed me some outstanding Rejected Children's Books that she wrote before she grew jaded and defeatist like everyone else. Multiple humiliating letters with each volume. Very fine archive. I have hopes that it will all come to us in due course... Now, Miss Ogilvie, do you have the framework for this morning's meeting?'

'Here you are, Principal Librarian. I have printed out one for everybody. No secret agendas here.'

'Splendid.' He cleared his throat authoritatively. 'Good morning, everyone.'

There was an unrehearsed chorus in response, mostly chair moving and coughing.

'Now,' continued the Principal Librarian firmly, 'before we proceed to other matters, I trust you will all have read through the detailed submission from our new Conservation Officer, Miss Winterhalter, which has been duly circulated to all staff? Perhaps, Miss Winterhalter, you would take the floor and steer us through the main points?'

The Conservation Officer blushed.

'Certainly, Dr Dr Patience. With pleasure. Mr Chair-'

'Just the one "Dr" will suffice, Miss Winterhalter, just the one.'

'Excuse me, Dr Patience. Well, everybody, can I say that the Chief Conservator has asked me to remind everybody how much we white-coats dislike leather bindings. They may look nice, but they're a lot more trouble than they're worth.'

She began to warm up.

'Why, a recent survey has shown that leather-bound books accessioned by us less than ten years ago already show signs of deterioration, meaning expensive treatment, if not, in the end, complete rebinding. Why –'

'I see what you are saying, as I think we all must do, do we not …?'

'You see –'

The Registrar interrupted.

'Hold it a minute. I'm confused, Principal. Are Conservation saying that we are to *remove* leather bindings on accession, or that we just *don't accept* manuscripts bound in leather, or *what*?'

The Principal Librarian nodded sympathetically.

'Neither, Mr de Butler. It seems to be common for people who find themselves left with manuscripts of our kind to have them specially bound in leather *before* presentation. This we should like to pre-empt if we have the chance. Our home bindings in inert, acid-free, alkali-free, nuclear-free (and wrinkle-free) materials are always to be preferred.'

The Chief Binder raised his hand.

'This is all well and good, Principal, but the Bindery, I have to say, is completely overwhelmed already. I need a couple of extra apprentices as it is, just to cope. Material floods in every day. Most stuff that comes to us is just bundles of typing paper, usually out of order, often with unnumbered pages held together – if we're lucky – by a rubber band. Sometimes, and I realise that the unions might have something to say about this, one of us actually has to *read a book* in order to put the pages back as they were meant to be. And with uninhibited modern writing that is not always so straightforward, especially with glue on your hands. My boys are often distraught.'

'Minute the extra apprentices,' said the Principal Librarian. 'Perfectly justified, perfectly justified. We can scoop up a couple of bargain-rate school-leavers with no qualifications. I'll have a word with the local Headmaster. Back to you, Miss Winterhalter…'

'Next, we are in a position to report on conservation research that has lately been carried out in the Department. Several curators had observed that unbound manuscripts coming into the Library are not infrequently disfigured by unsightly stains about the pages, particularly at the beginnings and the ends. Some months ago we were asked to try and remove these. Before we could undertake safe removal it was necessary for us to identify, if possible, what those stains were. Accordingly, a sampling of affected sheets was selected by a Conservation Research Scientist working closely with one of us, to form the subject of a primary nucleus of a working investigative programme, or WIP. This, of course, represents merely a pilot scheme, in advance of –'

'Er-… Miss Win-'

'… and *then*,' she continued firmly, 'the sheets were indexed on computer to allow accurate replacement, because we in Conservation have no time to read books either. We're just too busy, too. I mean, I wouldn't actually mind at all myself, but-'

'Might I suggest that we ask Mr Scranton at this point to summarise his findings for us?'

Obediently the Chief Research Officer began reading in a relentless technical drone from a prepared report lying on his knees.

'The sample sheets were subjected to a series of standardised investigative procedures, including Carbon 14, Carbon 15, Spectrographic Analysis, Electron Microscopy, Nuclear Activation and Looking. Identification tests were orientated in four primary dimensions, most lucidly categorized as up, down, this way and that. Our primary finding (or PF) was that all the stains were organic in nature.'

The Principal Librarian leaned back comfortably, as if this particular abbreviation conformed entirely to his own daily usage.

'P.F. Ah-hah.'

'Our *secondary* investigations, however, allowed something of a closer refinement.'

'Or C.R? And what was that, Mr Scranton?'

'4.45% of the samples contained haemoglobin, 62.86% were human dermal excreta, and 32.68% were predominantly saline solution.'

The Deputy Principal Librarian leaned forward in excitement.

'*Blood, sweat and tears, you mean?*'

'Exactly how we interpreted it in the lab.'

The Principal Librarian rubbed his hands.

'*Fascinating.* Does this not show us something of the manifest pangs of authorship, in a uniquely tangible and eloquent form?'

'To be scientific about it, it represents the manifest pangs of unpublished authorship at work, prior to Rejection.'

'Indeed, indeed. There is something here for a formal scholarly paper, surely?'

The Research Scientist looked thoughtful.

'Well, obvious lines of investigation are the ratio of spilled blood to excreted sweat in, say, poetry as opposed to literature, or possibly biography as against autobiography. One line that would interest me in particular would be the tracing of a possible relationship between blood groups and literary creativity. My colleague has suggested that it might be possible to reconstruct authors' dietary patterns from sweat analysis using sophisticated techniques developed recently in the States. If, of course, we can raise sponsorship from the private sector. This would, I think, Principal, be meat and drink for the literary historian?'

'I should say so. This is really exciting. There is no predictable limit to what we might discover. I wonder if we could cozen another British library into undertaking parallel research on some "successful" manuscripts from the nineteenth or eighteenth centuries?'

Miss Ogilvie, recalling her own girlish studies, was quick to intervene.

'Or even earlier, Principal. Think of Chaucer, or the Venerable Bede. What did he prefer for breakfast, one wonders?'

'We could start a data case,' said the Principal Librarian, triumphantly.

The Research Scientist spoke on, confidingly.

'It's early days yet, and I certainly wouldn't like you to pin me down, but since we're all here sharing I can also tell you that it looks as if some of our authors *might* be... *left-handed*. But don't quote me on that.'

'Wonderful. Remarkable. Pure science,' said the Principal Librarian, admiringly. It was exhilarating to feel so proud of one's people. He felt an unaccustomed surge of affection towards them all.

The Deputy Principal Librarian decided it was time to bring things down to earth.

'Correct me if I'm wrong, but while you've all been chatting I've been doing some calculations. When I was at school, I rather think that 4.45% plus 62.86% plus 32.68% made 99.99%. Isn't there a shortfall of 0.01%? Could you say something about that, Mr Scranton?'

The Research Scientist rustled his papers.

'Let me see ... Oh, yes ... here we are ... 0.01% ... here it is: "unidentified."'

'Can I just ask,' persisted the Deputy, 'whether that 0.01% is made up of, as it were, a single instance, or is there a sprinkling of separate deposits across your sample?'

'As I recall it's one instance of sequential blobs.'

The Principal Librarian resumed command.

'Well, does that wrap up science for this morning?'

'We think so, Principal.'

He beamed paternally at them all.

'Well. I have a little surprise for *you*. I have received a letter from my counterpart in California at the "Home of Handwritten Happenings" which includes a rather intriguing proposal. There is a young woman on his staff who has been carrying out some very innovative research, of a type that has never yet been undertaken in the United Kingdom. To *my* knowledge, that is.'

'We are on the edge of our seats, Principal.'

Miss Ogilvie spoke impulsively, but she spoke for them all.

'The point is this. Their manuscript library has an ongoing problem with silver-fish. It is these silver-fish that she has undertaken to investigate. As you will all know, previous research has focused on what glues they prefer, or what type of binder's cloth. In a pioneering new scheme this young woman has been trying to find out about their taste in *literature*.'

'But why should she come *here*?' asked Miss Winterhalter at length. 'There are no silver-fish in this Library, at least I don't believe that we have a problem with them. I've never actually come upon a silver-fish here, have you, Mr Scranton?'

'I thought I did once, but it was a fragment of tinsel from an old Christmas decoration. I agree that she's likely to have nothing to do.'

'Her name is Mary-Beth Schumacher. She will willy-nilly be here for the three months before Christmas as an intern in your department, Mr Scranton. Let us hope, then, that she finds something to occupy herself with in that time.'

Millie came in then with the tea trolley.

'Ah,' said the Principal Librarian, 'Just what we need.'

The Deputy Librarian seized his opportunity.

'Principal, may I air a problem which has loomed over us more than once recently that concerns the very vitals of our Library and its workings?'

'By all means, Sigurd. You sound most alarming.'

'The problem, as I see it, could *be* alarming. We are here, as you all know of course, to accept and preserve for the future manuscripts that no publisher would accept for publication. This is our task. In most cases incoming materials will be accompanied by rejection letters that give a taste of the author's experience at the hands of agents and publishers. Sometimes it is just a selection, to give the flavour, in other cases it is something more voluminous. The record to date is something over two thousand items, is it not, Mr de Butler?'

'Two thousand and seventy-three it is, Dr Sorensen, stretching over a complete non-career of "fruitless" activity. This was a rare case when the would-be author kept every specimen, right from the outset, as if sensing that this institution would one day come into existence and be grateful for them.'

'I suppose that many disappointed writers must simply tear such letters up with a snarl of literary rage and hurl them into the waste-paper basket, perhaps with a gesture of literary defiance?' remarked the Principal Librarian. 'I had never thought the mechanics through before, somehow.'

'Such a response is, I believe, commonplace, although variations in the details remain as yet an untouched field for the psychologist. Once we had a donation accompanied by a polythene bag full of brittle scraps of yellowing paper. On examination they all proved to be savaged R.L.'s.'

'R.L.'s?' murmured Dr Patience.

The Registrar nodded respectfully.

'Reject Letters. The thing was, they had been shredded *into* the bag, and preserved in that disembodied state. A unique case. It took one of Miss Winterhalter's predecessors about six months to put them back together again. Pieces of one typewritten word had been completely lost, but we worked out that it must have been "non-negotiable." The word was restored in pencil by Conservation, imitating the script of the

original typewriter, but in such a way as to be clearly visible *as* a restoration.'

'Thank you, Registrar,' said the Deputy. 'Anyway, this is my conundrum. Sometimes we have been given manuscript novels or poetry collections that date from early in an Unsuccessful Writer's career. The difficulty arises if the author achieves unlooked-for success late in life. This can lead to ruthless publishers grubbing around for "overlooked" or "unappreciated" early products in which the initiate can detect the hand of the incipient master already at work. This scenario could very well lead to one of our holdings being... belatedly ...- and I hate to use the word – *published.*'

There was a hiss of shock all round the table.

'Great Scott, Sigurd,' said the Principal Librarian. He had whitened perceptibly.

'Exactly. It's likely to be rare enough, but the possibility is there.'

Miss Ogilvie, not looking up from her stenographer's pad, was perturbed to notice that her leader's voice was slightly hoarse.

'Does anyone here have a response to this?'

'I suppose we just always take it for granted that the copy that comes to us is the only one that exists,' said the Registrar.

'If that has been the case up till now, I think changes will have to be instituted,' said the Deputy. 'We will just have to tighten up all round. Dr Patience?'

'Can we not stipulate that all other copies must be destroyed before we accept a given piece of work? Ask, in fact, for a written guarantee?'

'We can stipulate, certainly, but we can hardly enforce. And what happens, say, in the case of a sonnet given in the heat of the moment to an adoring mistress, who later proudly quotes it in full in her *Memoirs*, and then years later it turns up here, included as part of a standard collection of wholesome rejected poetry?'

The Principal Librarian sighed.

'Tricky one. Looks like gentleman's-agreement country to me.'

'Phooey! Let us not forget whom we are dealing with, Principal: *agents and publishers, agents and publishers!*'

'True. I rather think I must talk this over with our legal advisors.'

'I suppose,' said the Registrar thoughtfully, 'we could develop a case-mark to cover this sort of eventuality. Such works could be retrieved and stored elsewhere.'

'I was thinking that we should need to develop an appropriate ritual, to be enacted in the Library itself. The disgraced volume, face down on a salver, should pass between our librarians in two rows and straight out through the fire doors,' suggested the Deputy Principal Librarian.

It was obvious that he was feeling it all deeply.

'Followed by brandy in my room, perhaps?' said the Principal Librarian.

'I think so. People would inevitably be shaken up.'

The Principal Librarian saw that it was time to lighten the atmosphere.

'The librarian's path can indeed be a thorny one, dear colleagues. Just to cheer you all up, a well-known literary critic has written to ask me whether we would consider opening up a corner of the library for "books that should never have been written in the first place."'

There was a ripple of appreciative, professional laughter.

'On that note I think we will adjourn. One would not care to overburden the minutes, eh, Miss Ogilvie?'

'You are always so thoughtful, Dr Patience,' came the reply. As ever, her silver propelling pencil had sped tirelessly throughout the meeting.

5

The light was just beginning to fade when the Principal Librarian stepped out onto the drive. There was a pungent smell of late autumnal wet leaves and the gravel was slightly slippery underfoot. Montague Patience was in what he liked to think of as an elegiac mood, and he wanted to savour it without interruption. He paused to light a small black cigar and hunched his shoulders asymmetrically inside his W. H. Auden greatcoat. Life was good, his ship was on course through deep but untroubled waters, and his mind was clear. The American woman would be over at the end of the month, and in due course he might be able to wangle some visits for his staff in return. It was half a mile or more to the double gates that protected them all from the outside world, and another three-quarters of a mile down to the village. He liked the background feeling that the Library was respected by the locals there – rude mechanicals, as he thought of them privately - without any idea of what went on within its walls; it was an echo of the town and gown awareness of his university days, and he appreciated the respectful way with which he was greeted – or even saluted – by older men in the village. Once in a while he managed to get down to the local and fall into kindly conversation with whoever was there, spreading the message at a suitably uncomplicated level, at one with people outside. In the same fashion, he tended to encourage attendance at the local church among the staff, seeing it as an additional form of public relations. The local vicar he knew fairly well from one or two local occasions; he had it at the back of his mind to expose him to some virulent atheistic tracts that he had stumbled on in the Library, which seemed to him such a complete dismemberment of modern religion that they were worthy of a far wider readership.

He stepped out briskly. It was good to smoke like this.

The Library was admittedly shaky on fire regulations and precautions, but the no smoking rule was heavily enforced, and in fact nowadays there were few smokers among the staff beyond Mitcheson, and Ffolke on occasion. Dr Patience's occasional indulgence was frowned on so heavily by Miss Ogilvie that all the pleasure went out of it when he was 'caught,' but she would have gone off to her flat by the time he returned, and he fully intended to make the most of it now.

Great thoughts twirled through his mind. He was wrestling head on with his ongoing nemesis. How could he sum it up? It was - only partly, he acknowledged - *What was the point of the Library? What were they all doing?*

Of course, he knew what they were doing, better than anyone. He was the Principal Librarian, after all; he had redrafted their Charter, twice, and had been fluent in defending the Library from the media, on the rare occasions when they had to accommodate them, or in persuading cynical charities of the visionary nature of their work. In some ways he *was* the Library; it was not unknown for him to stand in front of the oil portraits of his predecessors and privately swear his allegiance to their work and all they stood for. Normal Library work was straightforward: it was the long-term purpose that troubled him. For that long-term objective must involve, in the end, some kind of self-assessment: important implications needed to be sorted out. Underneath it all, he was beginning to think, throbbed the insistent, perpetual unsatisfied question: *Was published literature any better than unpublished literature?*

And if that question could not be ignored, how would he, spokesman-in-chief at whose door this particular buck stopped and put down roots, undertake to answer it?

His intellectual upbringing said that there was only one way, and that was *scientifically*. Thank you so much. And where did science get him? *Definitions, Montague, definitions.* What, in other words, were the *differences* between published and unpublished literature? Well, published literature was always completely finished, and unpublished literature often not quite. That was true. Unpublished literature was often rough-hewn, poorly-spelled, uncorrected, repetitive, cliché-ridden, derivative, imitative, predictable, poor at the beginning, saggy in the middle and inept at the end, but there again so was the greater part of the recent published literature that he seemed to encounter nowadays. Not Dickens, okay, or Wilkie Collins or Thomas Hardy. But there weren't writers like that today, were there? Okay, trendy writers got their millions in advance, but, as his old tutor used to remark, *Who would be reading them bastards in a hundred years?* No-one. But look, giants didn't come into this discussion. They were different. Writing by *non*-giants was his territory. Writing by everybody *else*, as you might say, some of it bound between fancy covers and bought by the punters, and some not. And as a librarian he was entitled to think in terms of a fast-disappearing hundred years, and how that affected values. Where then stood the border between published and non-published non-giants?

And what about *editors*? Armies of editors, equipped with their surgical blue pencils, existed to convert the raw material of the unpublished author into the slick product needed by the trade, often reducing a new or original voice to muzak in the process. If he pursued this argument, a true *literatus* would say that his own manuscript holdings on some level were purer and more precious than the contents of all the public libraries and high-street bookshops piled up together.

The big difference between the mountain outside his Library and the growing one inside, then, was the hand of Commerce. The spotlight of commercial method, he would bet, could be profitably turned on any random novel in his safekeeping. With the benefit of cosmetic surgery, genetic engineering and professional publicity maybe any random manuscript could emerge as a successful product to join the dance queue in its turn. It was tempting, in fact, to consider trying an experiment. There was ample salacious literature of all types at his disposal, swerving from supposed autobiography to frankly actionable pornography; something from around the middle of the spectrum might do the trick. A catchy title, a good cover, a couple of Mafia-negotiated reviews or a bribed BBC interview and it would be on its way. Might even scoop up a prize. Surely a set of controlled experiments of this kind would constitute scientific method?

Say they selected six volumes with the worst possible R.L's (he felt good slipping into their jargon) in a mixture of genres – maybe two fiction, one poetry-collection, one historical novel, one *souvenir-de-sexe*, and really push the boat out on behalf of each. It would be wonderful to write up an account if one of them really made it big, juxtaposing the most destructive rejection with the most fulsome review. He chuckled to himself as he strode on.

There might be a way, too. Five miles beyond the village in the opposite direction lived a small, private publisher... *Hmm* ....

But could he square such experimentation with his colleagues? There could be no more heinous offence for him than to *publish* something in their care; it would transgress at least three clauses in the Charter simultaneously. The Trustees would have to fire him. Unless he could plead that it was scientific enquiry. Or, of course, unless no-one found out...

Dr Patience came to a fork in the drive. The left path curved away to cross the sluggish river that wound through the estate, leading to a second, much smaller gate beyond the copse. He wouldn't go down to the village; he needed solitude and darkness. He was in a mood to chuck meditative pebbles into water. He tossed the end of the cigar into the night and by force of habit took a peppermint from another pocket. Damn it, no. A second cigar was in order. He was on to something here.

The private publisher he was thinking of was very rich. He made his living in the unsavoury world of *vanity publishing*.

This atrocious practice unsettled everybody at the Last Resort Library whenever they met up with it, and the very term was forbidden in general conversation. It was, in a real sense, a direct challenge to them, stealing Rejected Material that was rightfully theirs, undermining the clarity of their position, and giving honest-to-goodness non-starters highly inappropriate ideas. It was all part of the modern world where traditional rules were being eroded. *Once* upon a time, as Dr Patience sometimes remarked in seminars, everyone had known what the difference was between publication and non-publication. But this *vanity* thing, when 200 "books" were printed off and all sold (or worse, *given away*) to the "author's" family, was *that* publishing? With ne'er so much as an ISBN between them? Not to his mind. It just muddied a librarian's waters. And he had heard of some infernal invention in America or somewhere where you put some kind of computer thingy in one end of a hundred-foot machine, pressed a button, and by the time you had cycled down to the far end there was a printed and bound brand-new *book* waiting damply for you on the delivery table. With this kind of diabolism you could have a *print run of one*. Was *that* publishing? As usual, the whole topic of unorthodox publishing made him giddy.

But this fat cat who thrived off it up the road was not such a bad chap in his way. He at least had a sense of humour, and owned two sports cars. They had bumped into one another on the train down from London and got talking. What was the blighter's name? Andrew something. Andrew ... *Caxton*. Yes, that was it. Of all names... Anyway Caxton had been very amusing about the tricks of his trade, explaining techniques for winning over the "poets" and "memoir-writers" that were his bread and butter. He and Posterity were on very good terms, as he remarked, and so he felt qualified to speak on her behalf. He had sample books which included particularly *sensitive* and *manly* fonts, and a seductive range of personal dedication wordings, in fact a whole rack of traps into which his prey leaped before so much as a pretence of a look. He was plausible, charming, and rather a proactive undertaker in manner. He knew exactly the moment to pause (as in the phrase "your … *manuscript*"), or lower his voice ("when you see *the book* for the first time and hold it in your *hands*"). Caxton kept a single specimen copy of all his publications in his house, partly out of a sense of pride, and partly because they were often useful in nudging an irresolute customer. He had graciously offered to show Montague his output, or even to drive over to the Library and give an informal lecture on his own aspect of the publishing industry. He wanted to call the talk *The Art of Pandering*, Montague remembered. He had been polite in putting the idea and the speaker off. His colleagues would have stoned him.

Andrew Caxton might well be the sort of person who would participate in a literary experiment, he thought. But he would surely not hold his tongue. He had been highly indiscreet about his clients on the train. It would be insane to trust his security to such a person. Forget it.

He strode on, puffing thoughtfully. And anyway, in real terms, what would such a plan prove? Nothing. Everybody knew how hard it was to get a book published. Newly-risen stars always tumbled over themselves to tell the press how many publishing houses had turned them down flat, seizing the chance – as they banked their royalties – to get their own back. People believed that there was a sort of *natural selection* in operation, didn't they? But his own question was this: did this natural selection process, heavily affected by commercial interest as it always had been, mean that the most meritorious literature always saw the light of day? *No.* The answer must assuredly be *no.* There was no divine steerage to ensure that all masterpieces fell into the hands of the perfect publisher. He, therefore, stood *in loco parentis* for pieces of greatness that slithered about with the others on the bloodied surface of the butcher's block, but slipped off the edge into the great stinking bin at the side, instead of being appreciatively topped and tailed, and wrapped in nice new paper for home consumption and enjoyment. Among all the lesser works under his roof there must be included many that were greater. After all, to follow the hackneyed argument, who would have published Joyce's *Ulysses* if the author had been a dumpy unknown woman with a wall eye in a plastic housecoat called Brenda Wilkins? Of course they all knew that, but "bring out your masterpieces" was not consciously in mind in his Library; there was a pleasing intellectual democracy among his colleagues. Many, in fact, preferred the "worst" writings they could find for their own reading. And, anyway, nobody would maintain that it had ever been claimed that all published books were masterpieces…

He picked up some mossy pebbles and tossed them one by one into the water. There was an itch at the back of his mind to get it accepted that what he – sorry, *they* – were doing had a validity beyond a mere "curious by-way of human activity" (as a journalist had once put it). They were a moral counterbalance to the frenetic philistinism of the publishing trade at large. Yes, that was it. *Moral safety valves.* So one day, when people wanted something un-regimented and spontaneous, they would be on hand.

Montague was pleased with this discovery. It represented a new twist to thoughts that he had gone over a thousand times. They were a sort of *garden centre*, then, with packaged seeds kept cool and dry until they were needed. Some were weeds, some were fodder, and others even exhibition roses. The Great Garden Centre. He smiled to himself. He hated gardening books with a venom similar to that reserved for cookery books, and had drafted a bye-law that Rejected Manuscripts in either genre would have no place in the Library. Dr Patience turned for home, his heart lightened. There would be something here to share with the others, with Sigurd, perhaps. Not yet, he must think yet deeper, but there was comfort in the idea that his Library, one day, would be acknowledged as a crucial component of the wider, eternal humanities.

6

The outer bell rang, long and hard. Stavros the Porter struggled out of his armchair.

'That'll be her,' said Millie. 'Ringing like that. Who else could it be?'

The taxi driver bent to the grille in irritation.

'Oh, there *is* somebody alive in there. I've got a female called Schumacher in the car, to be delivered to your boss, Dr Director. He in? Been driving round half the county looking for this place.'

'Oh, that's all right, I'll take charge. She's expected.'

It was always good to have it confirmed that the Library was hard to find. He must remember to tell Dr Patience.

He opened the door and stepped out into the wind. A tall, noisy-looking woman with a lot of hair wearing a malodorous-looking coat stood there while the taxi driver grumpily off-loaded a surprising number of suitcases and stacked them under the awning of the gate-house.

'Coo, what a lot of luggage,' said Stavros. 'Best leave it here for the moment, Miss. It will be perfectly safe.'

'Yes, well, I've come straight from the plane. Please be especially careful with that package you're holding. It contains glass.'

'We're very experienced here, Miss. Even with glass. Let me get through to the Principal Librarian.'

Stavros manoeuvred the bulky new walkie-talkie out of his jacket and fiddled with the knobs for slightly longer than was necessary. There was a convincing crackling, and he spoke urgently into the mouthpiece:

'Reporting in, Principal, from the gate-house.'

He turned his back and bent over slightly, as if monitoring his wavelength. There was a sound in response. Dr Patience kept his own walkie-talkie on a side table in his room, on a

state of ready alert. He was rather proud of them, and had toyed with a plan to issue hand-pieces to all senior staff, but had been persuaded by Miss Ogilvie that for anything indoors the internal telephone system was perfectly adequate.

'Your anticipated Mary-Beth Schumacher is arrived, Sir.'

'Is she within earshot?'

'Not quite. Bit of a handful I'd say, Sir.'

'Much as we feared. Well, thanks for the warning, Stavros.'

The Porter straightened up, and shouted 'Roger, Sir. Over and out, Sir,' and carefully put his apparatus away.

'Now, follow me carefully, Madam. We can't have you getting lost on your first morning.'

He had decided that the longest possible route was the one to go for.

'It's rather like a prison here, isn't it?' said Mary-Beth after a while. She had an American accent for sure, Californian in fact, as Stavros was accurately deducing.

'Depends on your perspective. As far as I can see we're not so much trying to keep certain things *in* as keeping other things *out*, if you take my meaning.'

'And it's very clean, too.'

'That's my Missus. Runs a tight ship, here, she does. Here we are, just up in this lift and we'll be at Dr Patience's door.'

The Principal Librarian was there to meet them as the lift doors parted. He bowed, beaming, and extended both hands in a vaguely pontifical way. It was a clever disorientating move, as she was discomfited by not knowing whether to shake hands or not.

'Dr Schumacher! What a pleasure! Welcome to our national Last Resort Library.'

'Well, this is a treat. What a journey. And what an amazing house. I just love the décor.'

'Come into my office and we'll have a cup of tea. There's plenty of time for you to meet the others. We are all always delighted to welcome a guest from our Sister Institution across the water.'

The driving purpose of their 'sister institution' was altogether different from their own. It was a completely independent set-up, and seemed to suffer none of the inhibitions and reluctance of the Last Resort Library. The management in California chiefly pursued manuscripts by famous authors, especially those of famous publications, and they had grown to become a world competitor in the market. There was, admittedly, one *corner* of their great institution that "offered a home to obscure and unprinted manuscripts," but their collecting in this field seemed at best arbitrary, and if there were an overarching policy it defied understanding in England. One irritating consequence of this fact was that publicity for their own Last Resort Library - such as it was - could never utilise the claim of its being, in the literal sense of the word, *unique*. (The crucial professional difference between collecting *any* rejected manuscript that you could get your hands on and collecting *some* now and again was not one calculated to make much impression on the casual outsider.) California sported a chatty departmental newsletter called *Sight Unseen*, and were even rumoured to be contemplating a full-blown scholarly periodical. The Principal's ribald announcement of this proposal in a meeting one day inspired a fine range of possible titles in his colleagues; the prize-winner was, unavoidably, *Unprintable Studies*. Ironically, as Dr Patience had established from old correspondence, the American Collection had been set on its path as the direct consequence of some particularly eloquent oratory somewhere by their own honoured Sir Bulward.

For these reasons the home attitude to the California operation had long been one of suppressed hostility. Overt hostility would not have been appropriate, especially as funding for exchanges and conferences was relatively easily to be procured from them, while alternative sources of such income from closer to home were practically non-existent. The Principal Librarian himself always had very mixed feelings about the other Library. For some time he had been hoping that in due course the Californians would lose interest in this side of their work and simply transfer their reject holdings to him but so far there had been no sign that this had ever been in their minds.

He had re-read the Schumacher letter from Los Angeles that morning. There was a paragraph in it, swamped in other stuff about exchange programmes, upcoming conferences, exhibitions and so forth, that he had not really taken in on first reading, but which now made him think twice:

> *... she is an unusual colleague, enterprising, energetic and full of energy. No problem is too small to engage her attention, no new field of research passes her by. We feel that she will profit directly from being closeted in your institution above all others. We will all, indeed, be the better off thereby.*

There was something under those lines, for certain, and his own instantaneous reaction on seeing her now was much the same as the Porter's. He swallowed down his anxiety. Suave diplomacy was always at a Principal Librarian's disposal, and Miss Ogilvie was doing wonderful work with a tea tray, and questions about the flight. He would get Miss O. to set her up in one of the guest rooms, of course, and Sigurd could show her round the library, and explain about her work space. He smiled benignly.

'... and we thought we'd put you in here, with the other white-coats,' said Mr Sorensen, opening the heavy glazed door, 'since you are a woman of science. It's not so big, our lab, but there are only two permanent staff stationed here at the moment. Sometimes there are more, and sometimes other scientists come, like you, and everybody squeezes up. You'll be sitting there.'

'You mean I have to work *here*, not in my own room?'

'Yes, this in fact is your personal seat. Will this area do for your bookshelf? There's usually a cactus here; they must have relocated it somewhere. And that's where we keep the coffee money. There's a rota.'

'I think I'd rather sit here.'

'That's Miss Winterhalter's desk, I'm afraid. She'll be back on Monday. Er, she won't like that at all…'

'Don't be frightened, Sigurd. We certainly do need some plants here, I think. It's just a matter of the correct use of space. Is this my computer, then? How quaint. Does it work on coal?'

'Actually there's only one computer in this room at the moment, Miss Schumacher. They share it. And I'm afraid that the printer doesn't work properly, so you might have to use the one in the central library or the Bindery.'

'We *share* a computer? You absolutely have to be kidding me.'

'No, this is England. But you do get to have your own rack of test-tubes if you're good.'

So, it wasn't an auspicious start, Sigurd reflected, and he was right.

Miss Winterhalter came back from a long weekend, happy and sleepy, keen to re-engage at the front line of research. Her first job, incredulous at the sight of her beloved laboratory, was to reclaim her desk, and sweep all the intruder's jumble into a pile, dumping it dismissively on her assigned table.

And it got no better.

There was the business of the personal files, for example. A day or two later Miss Winterhalter spent her lunch-hour printing off certain files on the computer and deleting them permanently. It was also soon necessary to explain plainly to Ms Schumacher that in England filing cabinets were private territory and the files within them even more so.

'What are you doing, Miss Schumacher?'

'Just taking a look around.'

'In someone else's filing cabinet?'

'Oh, that. I was just interested to see what goes on here. *Re*search projects, you know.'

'But those are private files.'

'Oh, that explains it. They are quite interesting...'

Mail sometimes arrived for her with an American stamp. Montague was all for intercepting these with an eye to unmasking some sinister plot, but Sigurd was adamant that such behaviour would be morally indefensible. Miss Winterhalter drew up the equivalent of an advent calendar, which made it painfully clear how long they all had to wait until Departure Day. Used days were heavily inked over.

A typed index card that Ms Schumacher put up in the canteen notice board offering massage and relaxation technique classes one week was at first ignored, and later defaced. Amanda told several people that she would suffer perpetual impetigo for a thousand years straight rather than submit herself to that woman's touch for a moment, and none of her hearers dissented from that view. Dr Scranton proposed injecting some very potent and quick-drying glue into her tube of massage goo that would set rigid as she bent over the victim before she could actually touch anyone. His animus against her was extreme and perpetual. Less than ten days after her arrival he had needed to go and lie down for a whole afternoon in a darkened room because of his mould samples. Months of careful work had been disrupted by an alien hand that, for some reason, felt impelled to investigate what was under, and behind, a tray of frond-filled petrie dishes. He had been virtually delirious with fury.

Nobody cared to hear about her research programme, or suggest new lines of investigation.

After a while no one except Rosemary Ogilvie would even sit with her at lunch. She felt it was her duty to do this sometimes, and it did give her an opportunity to keep an eye on her.

Even the Principal Librarian was vulnerable. Being seated regally behind his immense desk at the "controls" by no means protected him from persecution. One minute it was her health insurance arrangements. Next she needed a private car. She would have clearly liked to drop in for tea with him every afternoon, and it took all of Miss Ogilvie's forbearance to handle this presumption with restraint.

Dr Sorensen had never previously quite taken the Principal's point that the library staff was a kind of family, drawn together and working together. He had dismissed it as the sort of leader's speak that he would eschew when the time came for him to move onwards and upwards himself. But now, faced with the long-term presence of this poisonous virus in their midst, he felt a new kinship with the staff under his care, a sort of parish responsibility mixed with affection and appreciation. The Schumacher was, it had now become apparent, unquestionably the Enemy, and staff members, pushed beyond endurance, one by one came to him. Sigurd, a stickler for procedure, had begun a file of official complaints. Two weeks into her three-month residence things were already coming to a head, and staff were reported to be visiting the village pub for liquid lunches, wandering back rebelliously late after long slander sessions. The canteen staff grew depressed at the widespread rejection of their cooking. Colleagues were even heard to be looking around to see what might be on the job market.

The welfare of the Last Resort Library was, quite frankly, imperilled.

7

Miss Ogilvie knocked gently on her chief's oaken door, and stepped gently onto the rich, plump carpet.

'Dr Patience, we have to talk.'

'Dear Miss Ogilvie, you have my full attention as always.'

'Dear Dr Patience, we have to act. I have just been speaking with our Dr Scranton. He is ... please sit down ... job hunting. He called me to say not to call the photocopy repairman out again until the Shoemaker woman has been put down. There is nothing wrong with the machine this time; he has removed a small element on the quiet because she has been duplicating everything in sight, including people's very private papers, when no-one's about during the lunch hour. He demonstrated it from something she chucked away because the ink had smudged. It was Miss Bickerstaffe's annual job appraisal form. Sigurd was speechless.'

'Good God! Harvey wouldn't leave us? He can't! He's irreplaceable! The man is needed here round the clock, Rosemary!'

'He alluded to the possibility yesterday. Little Miss Winterhalter is on sick leave *again* this afternoon. She bears the brunt of it all, you know. Dr Scranton just retreats to the basement somewhere. He's developed some hush-hush long-term research project that requires special conditions. Isolation is high on the list. Sigurd believes he's manufacturing a small bomb.'

'She is driving me potty as well you know, Rosemary. She's on the phone to me ten times a day. The ladies' lavatory *this*. New apparatus *that*. No wonder the Californians despatched her over here. They've probably been partying hysterically over there since the moment she left. What on earth shall we do?'

'We must *act*, Principal. Call a secret meeting. There are some first rate brains in this Library. Use them! And I

have my father's pistol, by the way. It is in the bottom of my wardrobe. There are still two months and a week and a half of her visit to go, Montague.'

'*Brilliant*, Miss O. Get on the phone. All senior staff to assemble as soon as possible. Sigurd will think of something, or Ffolke. He's good with offensive tactics. I will *not* have my staff upset. We'll meet here behind a locked door. I'll get Stavros to circulate it that my office is closed that day for …'

'Pest control?'

'Good, but not, I think, good enough. She would insist that she had a right to participate.'

'Re-carpeting?'

'Better. Actually, that's a good idea. I am a bit fed up with this colour, now you mention it…'

Miss Ogilvie turned to her telephone. There was no need for her to look up any of the numbers, and the matter was rapidly resolved.

'It's all arranged. They'll all slide in here at ten to ten tomorrow morning. Madam probably won't have appeared by then anyway. And we'll think of something. Now look, Principal, we cannot have you depressed and down at heart. Would you like me to read you some new rejection letters? The librarians have been submitting real winners. There's a corker here from Mr Grubb in Novels, for example.'

'Do. I feel better already.'

'Here we go then:

> *Dear Sir,*
> *I write concerning the manuscript which you kindly submitted to us eleven months ago, which I have now looked over as promised.*
> *I adjudge your novel to be utterly devoid of interest, merit, appeal, humour, life or any other quality customarily regarded as mandatory within the publishing trade.*
> *You manifestly command neither grammar nor syntax, character construction nor dialogue, sense of pace nor*

*feel for atmosphere, rudiments of tension nor grasp
of reality. You lack any sense of drama nor indeed
understanding of the world. Your plotting leaks. Your
dialogue creaks*

*However, this is only my opinion, and I would like to
thank you on behalf of the company for thinking of us.
We would like to wish you every success in placing your
manuscript (here included) elsewhere.'*

'A choice representative of a widespread and influential school. Let it be known, Rosemary, that I will spice up this venture by offering prizes for the best entry under several headings. I am seeking outstanding examples of the following hallmarks: Blindness, Rudeness, Complacency, Hypocrisy and Arrogance. There will be additional awards for the letter with the most clichés, and maybe that with the most inappropriate spelling mistakes, disregarding millennium with one "n" or grammar with "er" at the end. What else have you on offer?'

'Something of a contrast, Principal, but also a well-known type, I think:

Dear Mr Peacock,

*Thank you for sending us your book, which we have
all read carefully. We all found it highly original,
absorbing, funny, entertaining and excellently written
and we adored the illustrations.*

*However, I am afraid we feel unable to take it for our
list at this time.*

*We would always be happy to look at another manuscript
in the future.*

And now, a true breath of fresh air:

Dear Sir,

*Our instantaneous decision not as much as to touch your
ms. may be likened to instinct, as when a blinkered horse
backs a way from a cliff overlooking a spouting volcano,
or a man in new brogues en route to dinner-for-two*

steps automatically and delicately round the side of a
pile of canine faecal matter steaming on the pavement.
D. L.

pp Blenkinsop and Hodges,
Lincoln etc.'

'Ah, the personal touch. And next...?'

Dear "Ever-Hopeful" of Godalming,
Don't be.
Just give up.
Sincerely,
Fat-Cat Agents, Ltd.

'Poetic.'

'There are a few to come from Poetry, but first two or three more from Mr Grubb:

Dear Sir,
We have read your manuscript. There is something of
a dispute here on the premises as to whether we should
send it back. A slight majority has argued that no-one
could possibly want to see it again. Could you please
advise?

and,

Dear Sir,
Despite grim experience of forty-seven years in
publishing, I am at a loss to comprehend why anyone
should want to have written such as manuscript as you
have sent. To say that it is a scandalous frittering away
of typing paper is not enough; you, Sir, are an affront to
any tree yet standing on the planet.

This next one is my personal favourite so far. It is from a postman, written in GPO carbon pencil:

Dear Mr Nicholls,
I have been instructed by the firm of publishers named
below not to deliver any more packages addressed to
them that come from you, on pain of dire consequences.

Part of those consequences are two pit-bull terriers which they keep on red alert in their front yard, straining and panting. I have reason to believe that at least one of them can read.

I must reluctantly request you (in conscious defiance of my Post Officer's oath of Fealty) from now on to deliver all such packages yourself.

'I love it. It should go on the wall. And what from our poets?'

'The first is from the Limerick Publishing Company, evidently a time-saving printed coupon:

The writing of verse is an Art
Elusive to most from the start;
Strive as you might,
Struggle and fight,
You'll never make good in the mart.

Then we have a personal rejection letter from a company specialising in love poetry. I gather that this has been especially favoured by Mr Payle:

Dear Sir,
We at this house stoutly maintain that there is a difference between the erotic and the emetic, and we have tried to preserve this distinction unswervingly in over two hundred years of publishing.
Your submission is thus at once to hand under plain wrapping.
Very sincerely yours …

Our final contribution has been done up in ink by hand on rather swish paper:

The writing of haiku is hip
It's pithy, and snappy and flip;
A syllable count
Ensures the amount
But to do it you must be a Nip.'

'You have quite cheered me up, Dear Miss Og. What do you say to a chocolate biscuit…?'

❦ 8 ❦

'Bar the door, Miss Ogilvie. We're all over here by the window.'

And so they were. All in a huddle. The Principal's senior staff in unparalleled, close-knit conclave.

'Now, you all know why we are here. We are – I think the term is - brainstorming. We need to find a way of getting rid of the Schumacher, before our - and I think I may use the phrase without fear of contradiction - happy family sinks irretrievably into a quagmire. I hereby admit before you all that I made a major blunder in letting the woman over the threshold, but who could have anticipated what it would mean? I am planning long-term revenge on the Americans when all this is concluded, I can tell you. In fact, I'll be calling for help with that matter too, when the moment is right.'

There was a groundswell of murmurs, among which '... for God's sake *do* something' was heard from Dr Scranton, and variations on '...another twenty-four hours and I'll ...' from several people.

'So, who has a plan?'

The question was forthright, and met with silence. At length, McTavish Bristow leaned forward in his chair and spoke quietly and deliberately, taking his time.

'I know that there have been a lot of complaints about this female, Principal, but I think our problems are unexpectedly over. I've got something that we can use to have her on the next plane out of Heathrow.'

'You are serious, I trust, McTavish?'

'Never more so. Let me elaborate. You remember the reactions of Dr Scranton and Miss Winterhalter when you mentioned silver-fish at that earlier meeting? How we none of us thought we had any? Well, we *didn't*. I know for sure. Because, over the last year or more I have been looking into all sorts of low life within this building, part of a broad survey that I've been conducting off my own bat.'

'You never mentioned this with regard to your Annual Report, did you?'

'Actually I didn't. I just got on with it in the odd free moment, first in the Bindery, later in the Stacks and the Reading Room. I had the idea of making a few recommendations, suggesting a few improvements here and there. But the thing is: definitely no silver-fish. I have no explanation for it, but I repeat that there are *no silver-fish on the premises*.'

'Go on, Mr Bristow.'

'Well, the shoe-maker woman arrives. Within ten minutes, we're all biting our nails and looking covertly at adverts for library jobs elsewhere.'

'*Don't*, McTavish, don't.'

'Two days later, Madam instigates her research. And what happens? *She finds silver-fish*. Quickly and easily. There she is, hogging the computer, typing in descriptions of silver-fish that she has netted in our library with no trouble at all. So, I had a bit of a think, and I went off to make a few investigations. And, nosing around in Love Stories, sub-section Happy Endings later that evening, what do you think I found?'

'I think we would all be grateful,' declared the Principal Librarian, 'if you would tell us without further ado.'

'At the back of a shelf I found a whole group of silver-fish lying out in the open, asleep on their backs as if they owned the place. I poked them with the tip of a pencil but they were dead to the world. And do you know why?'

Several of his colleagues asked why without hesitation.

'*Jet lag*. They were suffering from jet lag. My guess is that she brought them over with her on the plane, and set them free on the shelves when no-one was looking. She must have been in a big hurry, and failed to notice when they didn't scamper off as good little silver-fish should. They are as American as apple pie, and she brought them to Britain and planted them on us. The woman's nothing more than a common fraud.'

There was uninhibited consternation and exclamation. The Principal Librarian let it run its course, shaking his head.

'Good Heavens! Can such villainy exist? What do you say, Sigurd? Is this not true wickedness? Is it grounds enough for us to get rid of her?'

'Unquestionably, Principal. It's just a matter of how it is done. I think first that a vote of appreciation to Mr Bristow here for service over and above the call would be very much to the point. The details should be minuted in full, I should say.'

Applause. Everyone was beaming and getting up to shake the Binder's hand.

'Now, team, the question is, how exactly do we handle it?'

'I have thought about that,' said the Binder. 'I took the opportunity to scoop up some of her specimens, and I've kept them in my workshop. They're living off a page from a pink-covered medical romance that I pulled out of the Pile. Microscopic analysis establishes that they are a Californian species of silver-fish unknown in these waters – I mean shores.'

'Indeed. Nice move. I suppose I shall have to have a quiet word with her here, and ask her to do the proper thing.'

'Drink hemlock, you mean?' said Miss Ogilvie, darkly.

'Well, either that, or just go home immediately. Preferably both. I'll do it this afternoon.'

'Why not invite her in here right now and unmask her in front of everybody?' suggested the Deputy.

'I couldn't do that, Sigurd. Damn it, man, it would be inhuman.'

'It's what she deserves, in my opinion.'

'Let's all go down to the pub for lunch,' said Dr Patience impulsively. 'Anything on the menu's on me! For everybody!'

They tiptoed one by one down the back staircase and re-assembled, unobserved, in the car-park. Stavros was asked to chauffeur them all down in the van and bring them back afterwards. He was only too glad to do so.

It was something like two and a half hours later that Dr Patience, on top of the world, summoned his Personal Secretary and instructed her to telephone their Foreign Visitor and ask if she could possibly spare him a minute in his office there and then.

'It will be a pleasure.'

There was a little conversation into the mouthpiece.

"She's "on her way," Principal. I rather gather she was intending to come and see you anyway. She wants a more powerful microscope.'

'Does she, indeed. She wants a good hiding.'

There was a demanding knock, and Miss Ogilvie disappeared discreetly through into her own chamber.

'Enter.'

Mary-Beth Schumacher came gustily into the room, her hair all over the place, dropping some folder or other. Why was her corporeal persona so irritating?

'Ah, Montague. Good to see you. Where *is* everybody today? I have been meaning to come and see you and am glad you called me. There are one or two things that need straightening out about...'

'Kindly shut the door. Now kindly sit down and be quiet. I have something of import to impart to you.'

'What *are* you talking about, Monty?'

'*Dr* Patience to you. In fact, *Dr Dr* Patience. I do not allow underlings to address me by my Christian name in this library.'

'*Under*lings?'

'Underlings. People I employ. People I can fire. Like I'm firing you. That is to say, I am banning you from ever passing back in through the doors of my Library once you leave here this afternoon.'

'I *beg* your pardon. What on *earth* are you saying?'

'We have caught you red-handed, Madam. We know all about your little tricks with pet silver-fish. It is only through my innate sweetness of character that you weren't publicly exposed in front of everybody on the staff this morning. I expect you now to leave my Library after high-speed packing and *go back to America*. If you do that, I have decided not to make a public fuss, or even to raise the matter with your own employers. What have you to say for yourself?'

'I-... I-...'

She collapsed on the carpet in a dishevelled heap.

'Jesus *Christ*! Oh, God... Rosemary! *For God's sake come in here!*'

Miss Ogilvie opened the door immediately. Dr Patience stood white-faced, wringing his hands.

'It's all right, Montague. It's all right, really. She's only fainted. Call Stavros on the W.T. and I'll deal with her. Typical female device. At a time like that. When you handled her so beautifully. I was really proud.'

'You mean you were *listening*, Rosemary?'

'Of course. I agreed it with the others in the pub. We weren't sure if you'd be up to total ruthlessness. But you were *magnificent*. All the little strumpet *could* do was faint. I think that will be the end of it. I bet you a bag full of silver-fish that when she comes round she won't be able to remember anything at all.'

Stavros came in looking efficient and holding a glass of water, followed by Millie, who for some reason was carrying a towel. Mary-Beth moaned and sat up weakly. Miss Ogilvie, all concern, was at her side.

'Where am I? What happened?'

Miss Ogilvie winked over her head at her Principal.

'You were just about to pop downstairs and finish off your packing for your lovely flight all the way home to California. You came over a bit funny. No proper lunch, perhaps? They'll all be so glad to see you again.'

'Am I really? Gee, I'd better get on with it. What time is my plane then?'

'Miss Ogilvie is just about to phone and confirm all the details for you,' said the Principal Librarian with avuncular kindness. He really had thought for a minute that she was having a heart attack. '*Any* flight, what*ever* the expense,' he mouthed to Miss Ogilvie.

'And Stavros, you could drive her all the way couldn't you? You could *put off* especially whatever you have on to help out, I am sure? Here are the *forms I mentioned*, by the way.'

He went over to his desk, swiftly followed by Stavros. He spoke quietly.

'There's a complete week off for you and Mrs B. on full pay with double rum if you get that woman through the gate at Heathrow and bring photographic and documentary proof that she has left the country.'

Stavros nodded. They moved back towards the women.

'I'll go and fill up the van, Sir. The Missus will give Miss Schumacher a hand with the last of the packing.'

'Ms, not Miss.'

Slowly, one on each side, the Porter and his wife escorted the wobbly Ms Schumacher from the room.

'Rosemary, the brandy. *At once.* Two full glasses.'

'Here you are, Montague. Drink this. It's all right now. She'll be back there in her own library before she knows it.'

Dr Patience subsided into his easy chair and loosened his necktie.

'Phew. Remind me, when the time comes, Rosemary. *Revenge on the Californians ...*'

☞ 9 ☜

Acquisitions for the Library were altogether unpredictable, and all the staff knew how the slightest flicker of interest from a potential donor had to be patiently and studiously fanned into flame. No-one wanted to lose a manuscript offer, and young or inexperienced staff were always encouraged to go to the Principal Librarian if they were not confident about best procedure. Even seasoned Department Heads might profit from Dr Patience's remarkable gifts in that direction, or have a word with Miss Ogilvie. Thus it was with the Cornforth archive not long afterwards.

The first fax said:

> *Do you want my radio plays question stop.*
> *William Cornforth Esq. stop.*

Miss Ogilvie phoned down to Mr Mitcheson and asked him to come and deal with a drama message that had come through.

His reply was straightforward:

> *If they are unpublished and have been rejected*
> *yes please stop.*
> *P B Mitcheson stop.*

Later that afternoon, Mr Mitcheson had almost forgotten about the brief exchange because he was deep in hunting for examples of unperformed stage plays of the type *Nelson Meets Jane Austen*, which had caught his fancy as meriting a general appraisal. He was thus slightly annoyed to receive another telephone message from Miss Ogilvie. Mr Cornforth was back in contact.

His next message read:

> *You bet they are, son, every one stop.*
> *I have the paperwork to prove it stop.*
> *You'd better phone me up for a chinwag stop.*

Mr Mitcheson's reply was thus a little blunt, especially as

communicating by means of their machine was always such a touch-and-go affair:

What is your phone number stop,

which provoked the response:

You have my name and address stop.
What is stopping you finding it out for yourself stop.
Call yourself a librarian stop.

Mr Mitcheson felt peeved, and without the gentle intervention of Miss Ogilvie would definitely have let the thing slide, but she quietly came down to his room some time later with Mr Cornforth's telephone number written on a piece of card in clear script. Had he not been kept on the trail in this way the Library would have lost forever the Cornforth Radio Play Archive. Oblivious to what was at stake, Mr Mitcheson obediently dialled the number.

'Cornforth here. That the library chap?'

'Yes, Mr Cornforth. P. B. Mitcheson speaking, Drama Librarian at the Last Resort Library. How are you, Sir?'

'Found the number then? I should hope so.'

'Yes, no problem there. You wanted to have a talk, you said?'

'Indeed. I have written radio plays, son. Many, many radio plays. Not one has been broadcast, or even accepted for broadcasting. A good number have been kept for a time, sometimes a long time, while they were thinking about them, but their thoughts always came to the same thing in the end. "No." Now the thing is, son, if you write books, you can send them to this publisher or that publisher. They can say "no," but there's always another publisher. Know what I mean? However firmly they turn you down, you can get up and fight again. Now, it's not the same with the radio. There is *only one radio*, if you follow me. I mean, the old BBC say "no" to a radio play and where do you go? I mean, I have thought of radio drama departments in maybe Australia or Canada, but I never had the heart. They wouldn't understand my plays anyway, as they have been called "quintessentially English." So I never tried foreign radio.   I mean, if the old BBC wouldn't take them – and they were all written for the BBC, every one, why should anyone else?'

Mr Mitcheson parked himself on the edge of his desk, and murmured something understanding. He needed tobacco.

'So that's why I have come to you, son. I am wheelchair bound, you see. Pretty much trapped in the house for years. So I have heard about five thousand BBC radio plays in my time. Radio 3, Radio 4 – the others aren't up to drama. That's why, you see. I listened to so many, that I thought to myself one day, "Cornforth, that play – I mean whatever one it was I had just been listening to – is no good. You could write a better radio play than that." And I was right. I could, and I did. And I sent them in, one by one, sometimes several at a time. Comedies, tragedies, satires, courageous experiments, modern classics, the works. I wrote and waited. I even telephoned. Always the polite rejection. They never say why, the BBC. No character assassination, or helpful advice. Just "no." Once I heard from another would-be radio playwright that he had heard from somebody else that someone at the BBC had told *him* that the BBC *only take plays from their established, familiar playwrights.* So where did that leave me? The only thing left is the competitions, or once in a blue-moon they advertise on the radio for new plays from new playwrights. I nearly fell out of my chair in my eagerness to submit material the first time I heard that. I think there were about twenty plays in my envelope, marked – as they requested – with the running time: fifteen minutes, half an hour, twenty-three minutes; I got really professional at writing for a specific length. I analysed the *Radio Times* over months to work out the most exact realistic lengths they would need, and I always put at the top of my plays customised aids, like "could go on a Radio 3 Tuesday in the *Prom Interval*," or "Best after *Gardeners' Question Time* on an autumnal Sunday afternoon.' All to no avail, Mitcheson, no avail at all. I got so expert that

I could do you right now a play for any number of characters of any length on any theme with fluent witty dialogue and a serious point made under a veneer of light-hearted interplay with enlightening sound-effects and hints as to the nature of the most-appropriate type of music and a provisional named BBC cast, but *zilch*.'

'Yes, I see,' said Mr Mitcheson. He had been fiddling with a box of paperclips during this conversation and it fell on the floor. He swore.

'I've written all this out,' said Mr Cornforth, 'and you can have a copy with the plays themselves. And my outline typology.'

'Your *typology*, Mr Cornforth?' This sounded more interesting.

'Yes, son. I tried to get this whole thing onto an intellectual plane. Made a breakdown of what the BBC considered desirable radio dramatic genres. Such as *Kitchen Sink*.'

'Kitchen sink?'

'Surely. Madge is at the sink, crying into the washing-up water. Eric is being callous. Her opening speech must contain the declaration "I can't bear any more of this," or words to that effect. A very extensive and fruitful genre. It represents a major component of *The Archers*, for example.'

'Yes, I suppose it does. I see. That is rather interesting. What other categories did you come up with?'

'*But Inspector, there's one thing I don't understand.*'

'What's that?' said Mr Mitcheson, puzzled.

'No, son. Keep up, will you. That is a genre. BITOTIDU. The twenty-eight minute detective mystery. *But Inspector, there's one thing I don't understand* always introduces the concluding paragraphs before the signature tune comes in. It is not unconnected to the category *I think you had better give me the gun before someone gets hurt*, itself related to the broad, catch-all handle *Get 'im, Sarge*! There are hundreds and hundreds of plays of this kidney, many of the finest examples written by me, as you will see. Then there are the Ibsen-type plays, either translations of dreary Ibsen plays, dreary re-workings of them, or just indistinguishable dreary plays that might as well have been written by Ibsen. Favoured for Saturday nights with pretentious music, on the assumption that a really good radio play would be wasted on anybody in and listening at that sort of time. Another exclusively radio category is the Let's-see-if-we-can-outwit-the-stereophonic-workshop approach. No plot needed, or any other traditional dramatic feature, just a sounding board for extreme sound-effects – tension on a submarine, nerves inside the womb, that sort of thing. There are many, many categories in my typology. I won't take you through the whole thing now; you'll be able to work through it yourself. You'll find everything in there. So the thing is, son, this is your chance to make a big splash in the radio drama section: my complete unpublished dramatic work for radio (manuscript and typed versions, including rewrites); all my rejection slips; my outline annotated typology of radio plays known and unknown (four volumes; manuscript) and an autobiographical essay in despair called *Making a Play for Radio*. It's all yours. I guess I will never hear a BBC announcer saying those longed-for words: "In *The Muzzle Man*, William Cornforth's new play for Radio 3, the part of the Beware-of-the-Dog sign-writer was played by ..." So, son, when can you come down and claim your inheritance?'

☞ 10 ☜

Then there was the business of the P.W. collection. Another rumbling explosion mushrooming out of an innocent-looking enquiry. This time it was an antiquated postcard depicting the Bodleian Library in sunshine.

It made Miss Ogilvie feel nostalgic.

Dear Director,
I have long been a sympathiser with your wonderful institution, and twice even peered tremulously through your iron gates, without the courage to tug on your bell-pull. I have a proposition for you.
A new species of unwanted literature.
Do I have your permission to write at greater length?
Yours in admiration,
P.W. (ret'd.)

The calligraphy was of a bygone age and a pleasure to behold. Dr Patience propped the postcard against his small Eiffel Tower (a gift from the Bibliothèque Nationale, inscribed "à notre petite soeur" by a former colleague who now worked there), and wondered what it might mean.

Dear P.W. [he replied],
We are agog here as to your proposal.
Do, by all means, write to us.
Yours,
M.P.

His reply looked sparse on the notepaper. Now one came to think of it, there were no postcards of the Last Resort Library, but they would come in very handy for terse communications. He mused on it: the Buildings from the grounds, say, or the Reading Room, or a glimpse of the stacks. There could be a whole set, even.

Dear Director M.P.
For many years I have been collecting English

*manuscript diaries. Rescuing them, in fact. For no one
else wants them. They represent the written thoughts
of normal, un-famous people. I have many hundreds.
Actually, I have never counted. It might well be
thousands. They are all over the place here in our house.
Taped together with good library tape, of course, when
they make a group.
I am an old man, now.
I am concerned for their future.
I want you to take them.
Might you?
P.W.*

The second postcard showed an identical picture. He must
have picked up a whole box of them, thought Dr Patience.
He was disappointed at the message, for he had been really
hoping for an idea that none of them had thought of. No
one had thought of diaries, certainly, but they were not really
their sort of thing. He slid the card over to Miss Ogilvie,
composing a polite refusal in his mind as he did so.

'What a *wonderful* idea, Montague.'

The Principal looked up.

Miss Ogilvie was smiling in an uncharacteristically wistful
fashion.

'Well, that solves the problem of what to do with them,'
she remarked. 'I have wondered about it, sometimes.'

'What do you mean, Rosemary?'

'My own diaries. Now I can leave them to the Library.
They will certainly fit in perfectly.'

Her diaries. Well, of course, Montague knew vaguely that
she had been a persistent diarist all these years, and had even
wondered from time to time what she might have written
about him. Nearly the whole history of the institution would
be covered in that fluent narrative. All the tantrums and
embarrassments, as well as the triumphs and high moments.
Would be damn interesting, when the time came ... He
suppressed so unworthy a sentiment promptly. There was a

good deal of go left in Rosemary anyway. Thank God.

'Of course,' she continued, 'if we do take people's unwanted diaries, we would have to have a clause to protect privacy for a set period, wouldn't we, say, thirty years?'

'Oh quite, quite,' agreed Montague, hastily. 'I was about to make the same suggestion.'

'The diary collection would make a perfect appendage to Biography and Autobiography, wouldn't it? I should think Ffolke will see the thing immediately. He keeps one too, you know.'

'*Ffolke?*'

'Yes, ever since his days as a tribal warrior. All sorts of adventures there, Montague. Sacrificial virgins, the lot.'

'Call him in for a moment, would you?'

Ffolke came in nursing a hot chocolate. He had a runny nose and looked bleary, but perked up at once on reading over P.W.'s card.

'What a wizard scheme. I never would have thought of the idea. *Grab* the lot, Monty. You can have mine, too, when I drop off, now I think of it. Good stuff there.'

'We were thinking of an add-on to your territory, Ffolke,' said Dr Patience.

'Splendid. Sigurd won't like this at all, mind you. He will say they have never been rejected for publication, and that anyway they belong elsewhere.'

'Even Sigurd cannot deny that diaries can be literature, though,' said Miss Ogilvie. 'And if no one wants them, isn't that a substantial enough manifestation of rejection for our purposes?'

'At a girl, Rosie. You've backed him into a corner already.'

'Why don't we ask this retired P.W. to come and give us a seminar about his proposal? Let him explain his vision himself. Then we can discuss it among ourselves and give him a reasoned answer.'

'Sensible as ever, Rosemary. We shall do just that.'

P.W. made his appearance a week or so later. The Seminar Room was much improved by its sudden bout of spring-cleaning, and Stavros even remembered to replace the light bulbs and ensure that there was a squeaky marker for the whiteboard. The staff turned out in full, partly in response to a circulated instruction, but largely because it had been such a long time since the last 'outsider' seminar.

P.W. was a bent old man with long hair. He arrived in a vintage but valueless car, and took a long time getting out of the driver's seat. He then got into trouble trying to extricate his walking stick from the gear-lever. He was wearing a slightly theatrical cloak and an unclassifiable hat. Stavros stood by helpfully in the wings.

'There's a suitcase in the boot,' said the old man. He gestured vaguely. 'My daughter put it there. Perhaps …?'

'Leave that to me,' said Stavros. 'That sort of stuff's my speciality.'

They walked slowly together along the gravel, P.W. unsure of his balance, Stavros trying not to reveal any sign of strain. He wondered briefly about the daughter's likely build.

'They're all waiting for you in the Seminar Room,' he said, as they neared the entrance. 'Everyone is very excited that you have come.'

His companion said nothing in reply to this remark.

People were standing around in the room in groups. Dr Patience came forward and shook his guest warmly by the hand, expressing his sincere pleasure to make acquaintance.

Stavros heaved the suitcase onto the speaker's table at the front, and immediately left the room in pursuit of a beer. There were two seats ready, and a carafe of water. P.W. bundled up his cloak and threw back the lid of the suitcase. There were rows of small diaries, packed as economically as possible, many taped in groups as described in the postcard. Miss Ogilvie came over and peeked inside.

'How wonderful,' she said. 'I can't wait to get started.'

P.W. looked up at her and smiled.

It took him a long time to remove the bundles and undo them. He laid them out on the table, moved them here and there, and sat down in relief on one of the chairs.

Dr Patience called for attention and started to introduce his guest. He got so far, and stopped. He bent down.

'P.W. I am at a disadvantage here. I do not know what your name is.'

'Pontefract Wriothesley.'

'Let us welcome Mr Pontefract Wriothesley, who has come to make us an interesting proposal as to a possible new direction for the Library's collecting policy.'

Mr Wriothesley stood up with his stick.

'Ladies and gentlemen, I have brought you, as an appetiser, some of my diary collection. I am attached to them all. In my house there are many others.'

He stopped, and drank some water. He must certainly be eighty, thought Miss Ogilvie, possibly older. His voice, however, was firm and clear.

'I have been collecting diaries, rescuing them really, for fifty years or more. What I want to do is to hand them on to you, so that you can continue with this work. When I am deceased. They are, you see, the true voices of people for whom often nothing else survives after they are gone. Maybe an injection or two into the gene pool. But not, usually, other writing. Probably none of these long-vanished people' – he spread his hand out over the faded old volumes – 'ever wrote a full-size *book*. In fact I have never met a diarist who complained about publishers or the pain of having a manuscript rejected. These wee books are probably their alternative.

My argument is that these manuscripts represent an equivalent to what you fine people have been concerned with here. The voices in them are remarkable. None of them, you see, has written with an eye to publication. For most diarists,

the idea that someone else might read their words would fill them with horror. Maybe. They are, or were, private. But in them the whole world is observed. These specimens run from the early 1700s until last week. I rescue everything, you see. Any diary you like. Since I began this work I have never so much as picked up a novel. Never needed to. The whole of human nature, as they say, is quietly recorded here. The prosaic, the ritualistic, the moment of ecstasy.'

Again, he made the curious reverential movement with a bent hand over the waiting diaries.

'The main thing is,' he continued, striking the stage suddenly with the end of his stick, '*people tell the truth in their diaries*. Truth as they see it, of course. Now, I ask you, of what other genre of writing can such a generalization be true? Not your autobiography, not tax returns, not letters. Certainly not letters. On the contrary. *I've been meaning to write to you for ages.* Nonsense. Why haven't you then? *I miss you.* Most unlikely, if you actually have to say so. *I think of you every day.* Seldom achieved. In any given letter there is usually only one sincere sentence buried among falsity, in my opinion.

But diaries? Alone at night with this sympathetic, attentive and discreet companion, out comes the truth. Confessional, purging, tortured or cheerful. All true stuff. Voices from the grave, their fears, their hopes, their miniature ambitions. Surely these words are precious, and are to be *safeguarded?*'

There was complete silence in the room. He had been speaking quietly, and was now almost whispering. He seemed to have been sent as an emissary by a conspiracy of troubled ghostly writers.

'But aren't they mostly dentists' and MOT appointments nowadays?'

One of the younger librarians spoke out bluntly, shattering the mood; no one turned round.

'Some yes. But what I say is, wouldn't a 250-year old appointment diary with an apothecary and a blacksmith be interesting to you? Or *enchanting*, even? Remember, especially you who are mustered under this roof, it will soon *be* 250 years later than now. Some of these diaries are already from remote worlds. Before computers, before the Second World War, before the Crimean, and so on. What might seem modern, prosaic and uninteresting to people *just now* will soon be the exact opposite. *Tempus* most energetically *fugit*, remember.'

'Can we see some?' asked Dr Patience.

'Why, surely.'

Three or four people, including Miss Ogilvie, came up straightaway. The small bundles of diaries in their various shades of faded browns and reds did look full of promise, and in fact spoke irresistibly to the archivist in almost all of them.

'This is a good one,' said Mr Wriothesley. '1796; a lawyer's diary. Always has a blocked nose. Doesn't seem to be married. Hates dogs. Suspicious fellow all round, I always think. That one's an unsuccessful horse doctor. Here's a guilt-laden adulterer. Those are a couple of obedient boy scouts between the wars. Here's a displaced German preacher wrestling with big questions. This one's a nineteenth-century mesmerist. That is a post-war mother, four children, no housekeeping, and a gambler for a husband.'

'Can we ask you, is there a *catalogue*, or any kind of list, Mr Wriothesley?'

Amanda spoke. Two or three colleagues nodded. It had been uppermost in several minds.

P.W. tapped his head. 'In here.'

'And how many diaries do you think there are in your collection?'

'There are 412 diaries on this table. At home, I reckon, probably three thousand, five hundred individual volumes, maybe four, of which many go together, of course. You will need to know exactly, I presume?'

'Well, could you help us with the cataloguing in any way?'

'I know where they come from, sometimes whom they belonged to, and once in a while what I have paid for them.

Sometimes one gets associated photographs or other stuff, too. Samplers. Baby's first hair. I have kept it all where it belongs. But you may not wish to, of course.'

There was an old cigar box on the table too. Amanda lifted the lid, after a nod from the collector. It was chock-full of old diary pencils.

'Do you remove the pencils from your diaries, then?' she asked.

'Oh, no. Those are orphans. I have picked them up over the years, wherever I could find them. I have hundreds of them. It struck me that they were an eloquent item of propaganda, you see: *Where are their diaries?*'

He took other questions from the staff as they came up and inspected his wares, but made no further attempt to command the attention of the whole room.

Dr Patience was uncomfortable at luncheon, down at the village, since their unusual guest obviously felt that an agreement had been reached about the future of his collection, whereas from the Library point of view the matter was not at all resolved. He had seen Sigurd frowning earlier and one or two of the others looking sceptical. He would have to get the thing off the *And-who-exactly-was-going-to-catalogue-it?* footing. For a research library, like a museum, *acquisition* was the main thing. Paperwork could follow all in good time.

'So, Mr Wriothesley, how on earth do you *find* all your diaries?'

'Ah, Miss Ogilvie,' he said. 'That is the question. It is the devil's own work. People throw them away, you see. I have heard this a hundred times. It's a sort of reflex. I have a suspicion that they are subconsciously scared that old family diaries are full of sex, or proof of old debts, or illegitimate children who might have a claim in a forthcoming will.'

'Might it not be that people just think other people's diaries are private?' asked Miss Ogilvie, gently. 'I would think that would be my reaction. One is sort of brought up not to peek at people's diaries, isn't one? And surely diarists write their diaries with the same understanding in mind?'

'That is true. But with written documents there comes a point when concern with the privacy of the dead becomes a matter of sentimentality. You wouldn't scruple to read a diary from 1783, would you? Or 1819? Or 1902? So when does the border set in? My principle has always been to rescue the things. They will each soon be too old for anyone to scruple about privacy.'

'I say,' said Ffolke – he had been very quiet – 'do you really think that autobiographies are always so suspect?'

'Well, many biographies or autobiographies are written directly out of diaries are they not, supplemented by 'memory?' The process often shifts the product closer to literature than history.'

Ffolke nodded slowly.

'The other thing,' continued Mr Wriothesley, 'a surprising number of people keeps a diary. People seldom mention the fact. And men write them just as often as women. People often say they are dying out, but I see no sign of that. I imagine several of your colleagues here keep a diary.'

Ffolke looked at Rosemary, but neither said anything.

'I never got beyond January 9th,' said Montague. 'I just could never be bothered. *Had breakfast. Went to school. Mum cross.* It was all the same.'

Mr Wriothsley smiled. 'I like those diaries. *I loathe Margery. I HATE HOMEWORK.* But your diarists get hooked in different ways. Often diarists beget diarists. But your grown-up diarist cannot go to bed without filling in the day's contribution. Like cleaning your teeth.'

'If we take this up, could you give us some practical hints about how we might find diaries too? asked Dr Patience.

'My best allies are house-clearance people. Once the vultures have picked over a dead estate there is always stuff left that no one wants. Knitting patterns, old theatre programmes, stuff like that. Those are the boxes where the diaries end up.

And they go straight into a skip. I have a small army looking out. They rescue them for me for a few pennies. But then I try every lead I can think of. I never advertised as such, though. My dear wife was always edgy about merchants or nosy locals trudging up our garden path.' He fell silent.

'Have some dessert,' said Dr Patience, brandishing the menu. 'I must say I think this is a wonderful idea.'

He looked across at Rosemary for confirmation. Ffolke, too, was persuaded, he knew.

'I think I can say, Mr Wriothsley, that we would be delighted and honoured to take up this work. Shall we agree, then, that we will find you a special room in the Biography part of the Library, and a lot of miniature bookshelves?'

'I'd like to see that,' said Mr Wriothsley. 'My diaries are secreted in boxes all over the house. I have never seen them all out together. They'd look beautiful.' He looked a bit melancholy.

'We will decide between us in due course who is to be our Diary Librarian, and send them over to see you. And you could give them further hints as to how we might build on your work?'

'I shall be delighted. I have been exceedingly exercised lately about what would happen to them all. Afterwards. So send me your librarian, and we'll have a lovely few days...'

Sigurd was waiting restlessly when they returned. Mr Wriothsley had agreed that it would be simpler to leave his first delivery with Dr Patience, and had driven erratically off home to begin work on his list.

'I'm sorry, Montague, but I do think we need to discuss this before it goes any further. Frankly we are not here all in favour of Mr Wriothsley and his travelling *mini-bibliothèque*.'

'Well, Sigurd, we have had a long talk. It seems to me and Ffolke and Rosemary, that this proposal fits within our brief, and that indeed we should certainly profit from Mr Wriothsley's offer.'

'But there will be no end to it, Montague. It may be literature, but surely not very often. And anyway there are places that do this already, aren't there? Local archives, public record offices and what have you. This sort of material is surely *their* province?'

'Well. I put that very point to Pontefract, of course. He tells me that none of them will accept just *any* diary, and they always have to have local interest. So his job has been, as he tells it, to rescue the manuscript diaries that no one else wants. Not even their families. Now, as a policy, that is not so remote from our own, is it?'

'I must say I still have reservations. If these diaries were not written for publication, they cannot be said to represent rejected material in our sense. And anyway, where would they all go?'

'In fact, they'd be a satellite state of Ffolke's. He has a small room over there we could possibly turn to this purpose, actually. Needs re-plastering, of course, and shelving. Small desk for a worker. But it wouldn't affect anyone else other than Ffolke, and he is absolutely keen on the idea. We might pull in a new research assistant one of these days who could take over Diaries as a sub-section, if we feel it appropriate. We'll see. But all my instincts tell me that this is a sound new move for us, and fully in line with our purposes.'

'Hmm. You're the boss. But I retain my reluctance, Montague. It's a bit like the Music Collection.'

'Well, exactly, Sigurd. They are both wonderful ideas.'

Christmas was approaching again, Montague realised with a jolt. The Reading Room would soon to be transformed for the staff party, traditionally underwritten by him with considerable generosity, after which the Last Resort Library would go into slow gear until after the New Year.

This year it seemed a dramatic presentation was to be offered, under the overall supervision of P. B. Mitcheson. The mimeographed leaflet that came round promised the live presentation of a newly discovered parable in the Library's collections. Wrestling with age-old morals and the Dilemma of Man, it would be presented in costume, through mime. It was in three two-minute acts, to be entitled

The Indigent Cobbler, or, The Hen that laid a Silver Fish

All staff members would be cordially invited.

Christmas tended to be an odd time for Dr Patience. Virtually all the staff escaped from the premises, of course. Stavros and Millie would be there throughout, since their status as permanent residents and caretakers meant that family, if anything, came to them. Not that Stavros in any way encouraged it. Miss Ogilvie usually went dutifully to her sister for a few days, and this year Ffolke was going to some unnamed destination in France but would already be back by the 29th. Montague had shilly-shallied over one or two offers from friends, but this year would find himself a permanent resident too. Not that he minded. He quite liked to wander round the building without its inmates, a parent day-dreaming in the play-room when the children were away. Also, he wanted to write. Not that he would have divulged it to the toughest wing of the Inquisition, but Montague Patience was, in the deepest secrecy, working on a novel of his own.

He had had a most original idea, at least, so it seemed to him. It was to be a literary and introspective novel, concerned with the very process of novel writing. That was nothing new in itself, of course, the screwed-up paper all over the garret floor approach, but such works usually dwelled on the problem of the departure of inspiration – the agony of writer's block. Montague's idea was a novel about a novelist who had the opposite problem, whose muse tormented him into non-stop writing so that the ongoing creation of the work and unravelling of its complexities displaced the writer's own life entirely. It seemed to him to embody a whirlpool of possibilities that could be teased out and developed. Not least, that bewitching difference between life and literature.

The trouble was, he couldn't get *started* on the damn thing.

A few days of solitude should be invaluable.

It was odd that Mitcheson had come up with this performance idea off his own bat now, since Montague had been musing lately on a rather ambitious *Christmas Presentation Evening* thing himself. There would be no time now to organise it for this year, but he had begun thinking it out. The concept would mean good fun for the staff while simultaneously representing a useful step in his own Greater Plan. Briefly outlined (as indeed it came to be in the form of a non-distributed memo for Department Heads), the *Evening* would involve the staging of selected works from the Library's holdings before an invited audience from the commercial world of books. A carefully-selected act or two from one of Mr Mitcheson's unpublished stage plays would be followed by a poetry recital put together by Mr Payle, and readings of choice passages from a variety of Library novel categories. In the background, or rather, perhaps, between presentations, a pot-pourri of musical passages resurrected by Dr Boehm from scribbled pages under his care would be performed by hand-picked instrumentalists brought in from outside.

Many of the Library staff derived regular pleasure from sharing truly ghastly discoveries with one another; the remark "will you just look at *this*...?" was to be heard within the walls probably every day, but the Principal did not want this occasion to be a hawking of the most extremely dreadful held up for ridicule. On the contrary, he planned the public exposure of works of clear and undoubted merit, of, so to speak, *publishable* quality. His scheme was essentially that the numerous London publishers and agents who would turn up for an exotic evening in a romantic champagne setting would say to themselves "this is *unpublished?*' and 'Montague, how can this *be?*" On their way home, driven by sober spouses or partners, they would fall thoughtfully silent, and mull over the possible implications. After a day or two of active subconscious turmoil he would hope that some of them, just some of them, might come for the first time since childhood to *question their own judgement.*

It was a subtle plot, riddled with hazard; the only point that seemed to him to possess certainty was that there would be good attendance if liberal masses of alcohol were convincingly promised on the invitations. But he wouldn't be able to explain to any of his people what he was really doing. For them it could only be escapism, or a bit of showing off. He would have to make unwitting tools of them.

He talked it over with himself at length. What would Sigurd say? Sigurd, level-headed to a fault, would doubtless hate the idea, deplore the waste of time and resources, and finally point out with clinical persistence that what he was doing was a kind of *publication,* and therefore illegal according to the Charter. This was a fine point, and if it came to presenting the plan to the others he would need to bone up on it very closely indeed. It might mean running up to town for an hour or so in Lincoln's Inn with Barclay-Withthers. The Principal had a hunch – nothing more – that performance in private to a closed number of people who were invited guests with no money changing hands was *not* a form of publication, but he would certainly make sure of his ground. Then there was the problem that his Librarians would probably want to produce the very worst sort of material to entertain their visitors. This would be the automatic response, but perhaps he would be able to make them see that this would belittle their work, without divulging his own, deeper preoccupations.

(The latest plan was in any case far superior to its immediate predecessor. This had involved sending one selected piece of writing of a chosen genre through the post to ten critical voices of influence. Their task was to read it through and say, after reflection, whether they thought it must be published or unpublished. A sort of wine-tasting operation, judging quality and vintage virtually blindfold. This plan seemed flavoured with inherent poetry to the Principal; he could visualise so clearly the sweetness of the moment when he would declare: *No, it has never been published, but by heck it jolly well should have been*, so that the "judges" would blanch or gasp, and resolve from that day on to serve Literature, and eschew Mammon.)

Music would be crucial for the success of his evening. Talking of which, it was high time that he saw Dr Boehm for a little chat. Dr Patience kept up the Founder's practice of one-to-one meetings in his room with each of his academic staff on a regular basis, partly to keep an eye on what they were doing, and partly to give them a chance to speak to him at length in private. This system was regarded as a significant element in the Library's intellectual tradition, and he had been neglecting Guenther.

Guenther Boehm was the only member of the academic staff who was part time. He was a short, plump, and immensely committed musicologist, born of an English soprano mother and German violinist father and brought up chiefly in Heidelberg. He had been a sort of small-time prodigy, mastering a range of classical instruments with ease, and able to interpret the most complex scores at a time when most children struggle to read the alphabet. He had eventually gravitated to philosophical musicology. Guenther had applied

on something of a whim for the job as Music Librarian, and on being offered the post had promptly negotiated the right to one day a week off, which he devoted to peripatetic music teaching in several girls' schools reachable by motor bike. He claimed it was always necessary for an academic musicologist to keep performance and human contact alive, and Dr Patience had found the argument convincing. In addition, the Music Collection was not the hugest and only increased its holdings spasmodically. This was something that the Principal Librarian wanted to discuss that afternoon: could anything be done to improve things in that direction?

The first thing that he learned took him very much aback. Dr Boehm took a biscuit with his coffee, and leaned back in his armchair. His catalogue, he said, was finished. At least, in draft.

'I beg your pardon, Guenther?' said the Principal Librarian.

'Yes,' said Dr Boehm. 'My catalogue. I have been meaning to tell you, Principal. The draft entries are finished. There are two thousand eight hundred and seven individual compositions for which we have scores, or at least the basic musical content drawn out in approximately finished form. I have subdivided them into the traditional groups, of course, chamber music, symphonic, operatic etc., and there is my index now nearly finished of opening themes, and lists of the solo and chamber-music instruments involved. That index is worth persevering with. Dennis Braine's hosepipe sure started something... I am finishing up an analytic companion volume in which some consideration of the implications of the material included in the catalogue is offered for consideration by musicologists.'

'But this is *wonderful* news, Guenther. My warmest congratulations, my dear fellow... A finished catalogue... Well, well. I think it is true to say that none of us who have had the privilege to sit in this august chair have found themselves presented with exactly those words before. I confess myself disconcerted.'

'Mind you, I haven't as yet done anything about the Reject books *about* music. There are rather a lot. Appreciation, criticism, *My Life as a Starving One-Armed Violist, I was Wagner's Under-Gardener* and so forth. Other highlights we have include a manuscript encyclopaedia of the first three bars of, supposedly, all known tunes on index cards, several alternative systems of musical notation, sundry hand-bound hand-ruled books of unused musical score on vellum, as well as endless, endless operas, *Lorna D. Doone, The Life and Work of Billy Graham* and so forth. But that won't take as long. Also, as you know, Principal, it is an interim situation only. New material can come in at any minute.'

'Could you say something about your view of musical acquisitions, Guenther?'

'Well, the position with Music is different from Literature. It is almost impossible for people who aren't card-carrying composers in *Who's Who* to get music published as such. Performance for most is a delirious miracle, but then the composers just duplicate the scores, or, in some cases, even write them out by hand. So we don't have finished scores that have been rejected, with letters saying "become a plumber," or "rub out the notes and give the paper to someone else." For this reason one or two of our colleagues feel that we have no business collecting music that has been, as you might say, not so much condemned as unsuccessful, as simply never submitted for publication at all. Some are put in for competitions, and these sometimes have letters with them, but they are usually sympathetic and valid criticism to help the composers, not drive them to self-mutilation and suicide. The prize-winners usually only get a twenty-quid book-token anyway. There is hardly a point of comparison between the disciplines on this issue.'

'Indeed. One of our colleagues confided in me once that as far as he was concerned we might as well start collecting homework books or old postcards, and the issue came up again the other day. But let's say that we wanted to face this challenge with intellectual rigour. What if we were to have a debate in which you needed to defend the validity of the Music Section? Not your *job* – there you have no fears at all. I mean the *principle*. Could you weather the storm?'

'I believe certainly. The point is that we all collect for the future, don't we? In my view we are ultimately concerned here with *overlooked* voices as much as rejected voices. In one hundred years the fact that some fat bigot said no to a piece of creative work won't mean anything, but what will be significant is what survives. Now my Section is full of really good music. Some of it really wonderful, much of it as valid as anything broadcast on the radio, say. It is not all derivative or trendy or artificial or written with a machine. Not everyone pretends to be Schoenberg. There is music here which I consider of true importance, crossing borders, challenging all sorts of establishment and anti-establishment ideas. When I came here I thought that this work would help me to elucidate the difference between avant-guard music and crap. Well, there is not much crap here, Principal. Just the opposite.'

'Can you hear this stuff in your head when you read it, Guenther?'

'Largely, yes, of course. Arrangements for bicycle wheel or a bath full of mercury are not so straightforward, however. Mind you, I have heard some of the best stuff in performance already.'

'What? How on earth was that?'

'My girls. I have been using selected Library works in my teaching. There is a trio for oboe, cello and double bass, for instance. Wonderful, dreamy, sombre stuff. This is the first theme-,' and he began a low growling hum, waving one hand as if conducting himself.

'Yes, yes I see,' said Dr Patience hurriedly. But this was remarkable. Mr B had already been doing exactly what he had in mind. And the vision of a podium full of schoolgirls bringing this lost treasure to life was enchanting. He would have to consider the implications of this carefully later.

'Well, look, Guenther. You have nothing to worry about in your work. I am one hundred percent in agreement with you. Just carry on. And do what you can to bring in more material. Scores, I mean. Whenever possible. Chat up the widows, and so forth. Go to concerts by really old composers – you know the drill. And push onwards with that second volume. Perhaps we could have a concert on the premises one day?'

'Boy, that would *really* annoy the others,' said Guenther, appreciatively. 'I'll get on with it…'

Dr Boehm of course sent over a musical contribution plan for an evening concert the following day. There were already draft programme notes, and he had considerately added the duration for each work in parentheses, stressing that these could only be approximate. Dr Patience totalled them up in his head. The recital would be very slightly under six hours. Bit of pruning to be done there, perhaps. Or maybe I should give Guenther his head and let him really do the job properly?

☞ 12 ☜

It was New Year's Eve, or rather, it was a good hour or two into the New Year. Montague Patience couldn't sleep. He and Rosemary had been playing an intense round of Scrabble when the Fateful Hour, acknowledged with due solemnity by the BBC, passed them by. They were enjoying a very fine champagne and the kind of rewarding conversation that only occurs between old friends who have been through much together. Rosemary had been pleased to get home. She had brought him a late Christmas present, a pair of book ends featuring porcelain Sumo wrestlers leaning a hefty shoulder from each direction. She had found them through destiny, she claimed, in a reject shop.

Now he could not retrieve that peace of mind, and was lying there unwillingly reviewing his lack of accomplishment over the last half-century and concluding in New Year style that his whole existence was characterised by failure and insignificance. He put on his bedside light and turned to a reject thriller that had been lying on a table downstairs. The opening paragraph described the pale rays of the early morning sun gradually disclosing the dead body of a man huddled on the floor of a public telephone box. It was called *Number Unobtainable*. The early plot, for all its weakness and style, was not at all soporific. Unpublished theology would be far more effective. He got up and padded out into the passage towards the stairs, thinking he would go down and find something else.

He stopped. Undoubtedly there were noises from below. A thump. A cough. And a very faint light flickering somewhere. He stepped away from the head of the stairs, and slipped quietly down the other corridor to Miss Ogilvie's 'front door.' He knocked twice, quietly but sharply.

The Principal Librarian snapped on the central light in the Reading Room, and coughed. Two men in dark clothes

stood by the Central Catalogue, one middle-aged, the other far younger. They were not, to his irrational disappointment, wearing stocking masks, but they did have woolly caps and were each carrying a capacious-looking cloth bag. Dr Patience felt himself entirely competent to deal with the situation. His dressing gown was of a fine heavy material and he had no feeling of vulnerability with it wrapped and knotted familiarly around him. Also he was holding Miss Ogilvie's late father's revolver in his right hand, low down out of sight. Rosemary stood supportively somewhere behind him in the darkness. She had assured him that it was loaded.

'Ah, gentlemen, did you write in to the Duty Officer in advance? I'm just asking – no problem of course – but we usually do request prior warning from our Readers, you know. We are, technically, closed this evening, hence the former darkness in here, but now you are here, can we be of assistance?'

The two men looked at one another.

'There's no money here, chaps. In fact, most of the objects in this institution are only here because nobody wants them.'

The older man sighed, and stepped forward. He was carrying a tyre lever, Montague saw.

'There must be something valuable here. You play ball, nothing will go wrong. You got any rope?'

'Rope? No, I don't think I do. Not on me.'

He heard Rosemary move slightly behind him. He didn't look round.

'We've got a manuscript about tying knots, though. Written by a midshipman. It's called *Easy Does It*, I think. Would you like me to go and find it?'

'Did it come with trial samples?'

'No, I don't think it did. But that would have been a good idea. Maybe that's what put the publishers off.'

'Do you always talk this much when faced with violent criminals?'

'Well, we don't have a lot of visitors on this floor, you know. Bit of an ivory tower sort of place, you see. But I'm glad to see you fellows, even if it is a bit late.'

'We're going to render you immobile and go through the place for readily transportable items that can subsequently be converted into cash.'

'I see. Well, none of the rooms is locked. Beyond ... the labs. But that's just for ... security reasons. Oh, and to stop the heroin drying out.'

'We don't touch drugs. Completely immoral.'

'Oh, I quite agree. It's just that we have to keep a bit on the premises to keep Colonel Leguid peaceable. Sometimes we more or less have to sedate him. The man's been a mess ever since his Malaya police work.'

'Colonel Leguid?'

'Yes. Do you know him? He's in charge of Security here. He has a rare sort of fetish for edged weapons. Especially two-edged weapons.'

'I thought this place was some sort of library or whatever?'

Dr Patience smiled tolerantly.

'My dear chaps, that's just a cover story. We are really a secret government installation. Surely you must have twigged that from the relentless grey of the outer architecture as you approached?'

'It was too dark to form an accurate impression,' said the other burglar.

'So what do you really do here?' He put down his own blunt-edged weapon.

Dr Patience paused.

'I think I'll have to tell you. Chemical warfare research.'

'Balls,' said the first man. 'The sign outside said "Last *something* Library." And it's obviously a library. We've looked in most of the rooms. Just books, typewriters, paper everywhere. Never seen anything like it.'

'All that's merely cover. You didn't go ... *downstairs*?'

'Weedon did, didn't you, Weed?'

'Only briefly.'

'I know that it says *Last Resort Library* on the board outside. That's a sort of Whitehall joke. L.R.L. The letters really stand, however, for *Lethal Research Laboratories*. We handle – well, I shouldn't really say but now we know you both it's okay – we're developing antibodies for use against, well, certain … bodies. You didn't *touch* anything downstairs, did you Weedon?'

'Ner. It was dark. Anyway, I'm wearing my professional gloves. Look.'

'So you are. Thank goodness. Rats that wander around down there seem to die immediately, especially when they've been running an experiment. We always have to wear the *full suit*, if we're not on duty up here.'

He laughed briefly, a sort of throwaway, brave gesture, then checked himself.

'We mustn't make too much noise. The Colonel is a notoriously light sleeper.'

'Look, you got a safe here?' persisted the older man stolidly.

'Uncle, I thought you promised – '

'Quiet, Weed. Okay, okay,' said the older man. 'You've got no petty cash? Travellers' cheques? It was hard work coming through that damn wood. And Weedon got a puncture near the gates.'

'That's hard luck. I am sure we'll have a repair kit somewhere.'

'*We do, Principal.*'

The new voice was a muffled bellow coming from the other side of the room. A bizarre figure wearing a huge bee-keeper's helmet and holding a giant iron spear of West African manufacture stepped out of the gloom. He seemed taller than man can usually be and adopted a stance of granite, his body at a fighting angle, the lethal point steady in his grasp.

'*Don't move. Don't look at him. Don't annoy him.*'

The tension was clear to both men in Dr Patience's urgent whisper.

'*Any trouble here, Principal?*'

'No, no, Colonel. Everything is fine. Absolutely. Not to disturb yourself.'

'Is that so? Then what are these men doing here?'

'Men? Oh, *them*. Weedon here, and his colleague – er ?'

'Swag.'

'You aren't serious? *Swag*? Bit of a give-away, isn't it?'

'Well, it's Arthur Dagenham, really. Been Swag since my first stay in the Scrubs. Years ago. I've sort of got used to it. After a –'

'Principal, in as much as I can see through this mesh, these men look decidedly unlike plausible readers to me. I would check their papers straight away. I think they might be Russian chemists. I submit that they are on the premises for other reasons than sampling our poetry. In fact, I'll warrant there are two parachutes somewhere in the grounds. Shall we rouse Stavros *and the dogs?*'

Millie, Montague remembered then, was babysitting her niece's two Pekinese for a month.

'Perhaps we should,' was all he could manage.

'Principal, I want answers and I want them *now*,' said Ffolke, warming to his role. It was difficult not to slide into an obvious accent. 'It's much too long since I interrogated an interloper. What say I take them out to the ... *shed*? Is the chain saw still out there?'

He spoke with a curious deliberation, if not relish, his spear quivering perceptibly with enthusiasm. Ffolke was contemplating a giggle of anticipatory glee, but saw it might be over the top. Rosemary, spellbound by his bloodcurdling menace, had unwillingly to withdraw briefly into the hall to go to the ladies.

'I don't mind, Colonel, if it's just one,' said Montague, reasonably. 'But it takes the pike ages to clean the pond up afterwards, remember.'

Swag and Weedon stood close together. Weedon was trembling. Dr Patience saw Swag feeling behind him for the tyre lever.

'Swag! Don't be a fool!' he shouted.

In a flash the grotesque masked figure lunged forward and with lethal accuracy pinned Swag's right sleeve to the desk with the spear point.

'*Yes!* The *speed*, the *skill*, it's still all there!'

The suddenness of the war cry made even Montague jump. His pacifist forefinger jerked convulsively on the trigger, and a venerable Ogilvie bullet smashed with a huge roar into Sir Bulward's favourite Turkish carpet. The noise stunned everyone except the Colonel.

'Bullets and steel,' he cried in a kind of dreamy ecstasy.

'Now look what you've made me do,' said Montague. 'Colonel! Pull yourself together. Not the new leather. I appreciate your thinking and swift action here, but it is only fair to tell you that Weedon and Swag were merely passing and wondered whether we had any - er –'

He coughed, not being used to cordite.

'*Yes?*'

'Books on bird watching, Colonel. By *night*.'

'Oh, I *see*, Montague. Well, that changes everything. Why didn't you say so *before*? We do have something, as a matter of fact. There's a very useful little manual from the late 1930's by an amateur who discovered he was colour-blind. He took up observing by night on the assumption that his handicap would make no difference. Do you want me to fetch it up?'

'That would be kind,' said Swag, still awkwardly captive over the desk. Weedon nodded hard.

Ffolke pulled his spear out carefully and propped it against the wall. He removed his helmet.

'Phew, they're hot, those things. I'll just –'

It transpired that he had been walking on some kind of wooden mini-stilts.

'*Snake skates*. I invented them. Damn useful. Won't be a minute. I think I know exactly where that book is.'

He went out into the hall.   Dr Patience put down his gun.

'So how did you fellows get in, so to speak?'

'We came right in through the front door. Wasn't locked or anything. I was about to do a window when Weedon turned the handle. He's a bright kid.'

'That front door mechanism is part of an experimental new approach to high-level security. Double-bluff thing.'

'Yes, I see. It certainly fooled me.'

'So you came though the woods? There are perfectly good paths, of course.'

'Yeh. Well. That was my idea. Cover.'

'You sensed instinctively that we have lights and trip wires and state-of-the-art security cameras?'

'We weren't taking any chances.'

'Yes, but there are also nine illegal Victorian man traps in the undergrowth,' remarked Dr Patience. 'Remember next time, won't you? Rosemary, dear, what kind of hosts can we seem? What about some tea?'

'Black for me please Miss,' said Swag. He sat down carefully on a library chair and put down his sack. Then his tyre lever. He examined his sleeve. Weedon was still white and shaky.

'Actually, Dr Patience, there's some turkey left, and loads of cake. I think I'll ...'

'Beneath us,' said Dr Patience, commanding attention,' are two very deep subterranean floors, built at vast expense and with total secrecy, with lead-sheathed rooms and shielded, silent corridors. Most of our staff live and work down there. There's a special lift. They never know if it's day or night. They'll be a dozen men and women at their benches down there now as I speak.' He tapped the floor. 'Doing their bit for Britain and Her Majesty. And the safety of all of us. But look, chaps, you can tell no one. Not even your wives. If word got out ... You've heard of the Official Secrets Act?'

They nodded.

'Well there you are then.'

They nodded again.

'As for you, Weed, burn those gloves when you get home and have a protracted hot bath with lashings of iodine in the water. If you get any funny symptoms, say your watch starts accelerating, you'd better phone one of us immediately.'

Miss Ogilvie came in with Millie's trolley.

'So is this your first job, Weed?'

'Yeh. God, I'm starving. My first breaking and entering. Uncle thought this would be a good opportunity to get some experience.'

'Weed, let me correct you there. Nothing was broken. You and Uncle Swag got lost in the woods, understandably, as it was dark, and you popped in through the unlocked front door to ask one of us for a glass of water. Actually you found tea and cake instead. Good night's work all round, I'd say.'

Miss Ogilvie yawned delicately behind her hands.

'Look, we must be off,' said Swag. 'You must all be exhausted. It's been a lovely evening. And I've still got to fix Weed's tyre.'

'No, no, take it easy. There's a lot of food to be eaten. I'll have to go and turn off the cameras if you boys would prefer to take the path on the way back...'

There were indistinct voices from the front hall. Ffolke came in holding a book accompanied by two uniformed police officers. He had added a burly sweater to his pyjama outfit.

'Dr Patience?'

'At your service, Sergeant ...?'

'Seth R. Lancaster. At 2.13 am we found two suspicious-looking bicycles leaning against - why, *hello Swag*. Well, well, well. And young Weedon as bridesmaid. *What* a surprise. Bit out of your usual run, isn't it, library books?'

'This isn't just a *lib-*' said Weedon. Dr Patience caught his eye and shook his head very slightly.

'Well, well, well,' repeated the officer. 'Looks like a dead to rights open and shut case of aggravated book-burglary to me, eh Brandon?'

He pulled out his notebook. Brandon grunted. He wanted to go home to bed.

'Let's have a look in them bags. Hey, can you smell something, Constable?' added the Sergeant suddenly.

Brandon turned the bags upside down. An open packet of cigarettes fell out of one. Nothing else.

'Weedon!' said his uncle.

'No smoking in the Library,' said Dr Patience automatically.

'Interrupted by the Professor here before you got started then? Anyway, boys, we'll be discussing the whole thing down at the station.'

'Just a minute, Sergeant. I don't think you've quite got the right idea. Swag and Weed are here by invitation. They were in the grounds, pursuing the first cuckoo of the year for the Society. There's a prize, you see. They're old friends.'

'Cuckoo? In January? You know who these fellows are?'

'They run Dag's Depot in town don't they?' said Ffolke, 'I've been in there many times. House clearance. I picked up a nice lampshade there a few weeks ago. Very reasonable, I thought it.'

'House clearance is right. By night. When the owners are asleep and oblivious. This is a typical New Year's Eve outbreak of breaking-in. All the villains seem to have a crack on New Year's Eve, and this is just a normal −'

'Sergeant Lancaster. Do not distress yourself. Whether these gentlemen are prone to moonlighting now and then as you imply cannot concern us now. They are here as our guests, as indeed are you.'

'That turkey looks good,' said Brandon.

Rosemary smiled at him sweetly and passed him and Seth plate and napkin.

'I say, Ffolke, on an occasion like this I think we can do a bit better. Will you hold the fort with our friends while I go down to the cellars?'

'Don't forget your *suit*, Sir,' said Weedon, in a panic.

'It's OK, Weed, I'll use the *other door*.'

'You keep bees, then, Colonel?' Sergeant Lancaster was asking, as Montague came back through the double doors with his arms full of bottles. Brandon was telling Swag a long joke with his mouth full, and Rosemary was looking over Ffolke's useful book with Weedon. The police officers were the first to leave, as the other two offered to help with the washing up.

'Nice pistol,' commented Swag, as his nephew manipulated the tray through the library doors on his way to the kitchens. 'Worth a few bob.'

'Tell me, Swag, you chaps ever come upon old diaries during your daytime ventures? If you do, let us know. Useful camouflage...'

As they crossed the moonlit courtyard a high-pitched, irritating, fluffy, effeminate, pocket-sized yapping could be heard. Swag looked quizzically at the Principal Librarian by his side.

'Chinese killer dogs,' said Dr Patience, confidingly. 'Specially-developed breed ...'

The first disruption of their calm in the new year started with a bulky envelope addressed to the "Poetry Librarian, The Last Resort Library," with the correct county added too. The postman had delivered it with impressive accuracy.

'Someone knows how this place works,' said Miss Ogilvie to herself, sorting the letters in front of the pigeon-holes in Reception. This humble task had traditionally remained her responsibility for years, largely because when the Library was founded virtually all correspondence had been addressed to the Principal Librarian. A good deal of the mail nowadays was for the rest of the staff, although of them all Mr Payle tended to receive least in the way of professional letters.

The Honourable Pomfret Payle, perhaps more than most of his Library colleagues, was considered to look the part. He wore broad green corduroy suits over bulky cricket sweaters and favoured sandals for the greater part of the year, indoors and out. He had a pale flat face with a completely straight fringe of blond hair and looked like an overblown and vaguely-corrupted chorister. He had abandoned a potentially colossal study of nineteenth-century minor British poets one fifth of the way through, contenting himself after college with being a very minor poet himself. There had been a scattering of short works published in magazines and a miscellany or two of new writing. The Payle had spent some years teaching English literature in a variety of institutions before stumbling across the advert for what became his job on the leaflet table at a poetry convention. His application had been one of a huge number. He had been short-listed on the basis of his name and the fact that he had published so little, but had been selected only after substantial discussion and delay. Dr Patience, who had inherited him from his predecessor, regarded him with mixed feelings, and had deliberately appointed young Louis

Brecknock in the hope that a little rivalry would be good for him. In fact, the presence of an Assistant Poetry Librarian with similar interests seemed to have no effect at all on Mr Payle, who persisted in his dreamy way of filling days and weeks in unexplained researches, offering little communication with his superiors or his inferior.

The new package contained about one hundred type-written poems for children, and formed what had obviously been conceived as a whole book. Mr Payle's heart sank. He hated children's poetry passionately, published or unpublished, and for all his refined sensitivity had a good deal of trouble in distinguishing literary merit in either. A donation like this meant writing an acknowledgement letter, deciding on classification and case mark, writing a draft catalogue entry, boxing the thing and, if he could face it, a skim read to allow the framing of some additional material for the catalogue. Somehow this standard daily work always seemed to him unmerited for mere children's poems. He had been thinking recently that he could cleverly make infantile poetry a Special Responsibility for the Brecknock pest, who would probably seize upon the chance as some form of oblique promotion. Good idea. A good deal easier than trying to transfer the whole lot, and there was a whole lot, over to Children's Literature, which had crossed his mind as a possible plan on more than one occasion.

There were the inevitable letters. "This sort of slight versification is best suited to family consumption, or to other people who know the poet personally. It could never be taken seriously for publication..." "Strained and artificial; immensely too 'clever' and adult; the writer should get to know some real live children before trying to write children's poetry." A particularly villainous variant of this one was, "This is an adult's idea of what children like to read." The author had written defiantly in the margin: *I have four children, and they, like all the other children who have read these poems, love*

them. All unsuccessful children's poets seemed to make the point that bus-loads of children who had read or heard the work loved it. No child enduring a poem by some uncle or a neighbour ever said 'fine for an informal occasion like this but if you're thinking of publishing forget it.' They all said *'more, Uncle Nicky, read us more,'* and adopted fawning expressions of awestruck appreciation. So this grass-roots endorsement did not add up to a hill of beans.

He leafed inattentively through the sheaf of Reject Letters, taken aback suddenly to find that the last and longest letter was addressed to him personally:

Dear Mr Payle,

I know what you do in your library and how you like the publishers' refusal letters as well as the poems so that is why I have sent you all this today. My children are grown up now and there is no point in my keeping this stuff here.

There is some corruption in the world of children's poetry that I want to draw to your attention. Two years ago I was sent by a poet friend a printed polychrome leaflet advertising a competition for new children's poetry. There was a woman children's poet, apparently well published herself, who had had the idea that it would be interesting to publish a compendium of completely new children's poetry by completely new children's poets. Her idea was that she would hold a competition. This would be like other poetry competitions in that you could submit as many poems as you liked, but it would cost you £4.00 for each poem. After the closing date of the competition there would be the judging, and first, second and third prizes would be awarded, and the winners' names announced. In addition, another ninety-seven poems would be selected from all the submissions to make up a total of one hundred special new never-before-seen poems for children. The book would be out within six months, and those whose works were included would qualify to purchase a copy or copies of the publication at a special reduced price.

The unusual and most seductive thing for me about this particular competition was that there was one extra stipulation (in addition to the £4.00 a shot matter). You had to be a completely unpublished poet. *Not that the poems submitted had to be unpublished, but you yourself had to be an unpublished poet, or, I suppose therefore, a still would-be-poet. I remember with clarity the jocular way with which I embraced this stipulation. 'No-one,' said I, 'could accuse me of unscrupulousness in that regard, ha ha!' I had never managed to get so much as a syllable published then, you see, so I felt supremely eligible, since a fifty-eight year old unpublished poet is a lot more unpublished than say a twenty-two year old one, if you see what I mean.*

So, I sent in eight or nine of my children's poems, specially typed out double spaced on separate sheets in accordance with the instructions, together with well over thirty pounds, a large stamped addressed envelope, and a signed document attesting to my totally unpublished state. Off it all went in the post.

The closing day came and went, and a long patient period was allowed by me for late entries, and judging. Perhaps the poems were all equally wonderful, perhaps one of the judges had typhoid, whatever. After three months I dug out the pamphlet to look for a telephone number. There was one, so I rang, many times, with no answer. One afternoon a polite young man did answer, and said that the organiser wasn't there, but that there had been a huge submission, and judging was now being finalised. News would come shortly to all competitors. No news came for a long time. Very much later I rang. She still wasn't there, but the polite young man was and looked up the results for me. He came back after five minutes to say that I wasn't a prize winner but that two of my poems had been selected for the book.

Euphoria for at least a fortnight!

Then, nothing. No letter. No proofs. The only thing that did come was an application form for the purchase of one or more copies of the book. Drawings were still being worked on then, they wrote, and the publication date had to be pushed back a bit.

My husband gently suggested that it would be premature to send them the forty or more pounds (including p. and p.) for the book. I didn't tell him that actually I had been thinking of ten or fifteen copies; all the children, a few grandchildren, and one or two Doubting Thomases who had always said 'give it up, Emilia.'

My husband also rang the number periodically. The same young man explained that the organiser had now had a miscarriage and was in hospital and would be recuperating for some time. My husband asked about the book. 'On course,' said the young man cheerfully. Julius tried I think once more. There had been a serious hold up, said the young man, the expense of the final publication had been seriously underestimated, and she was now thinking of trying to raise funding to see it through the press. 'What about the money from subscribers?' asked my husband. 'It's all in the bank,' said the young man blithely, 'and we've got records of everyone's addresses so it's all right.' My husband put the phone down then and we went out to dinner.

The enclosed papers include the original publicity and entry form and everything that I have received from these people. My husband and I think it unlikely that the promised volume will appear in our lifetimes. Or anyone else's.

If it is in your power to do anything to deal with them,
and keep other poor completely unpublished poets
(YOUR BIGGEST FANS) out of their clutches, please
do so.
Yours truly.

                                    Emilia Stokrotka.

Mr Payle was affected in complex ways on reading this. He registered sincere sympathy for Emilia, who anyone could see was clearly a decent woman. A sad case. But as a *scam*, though, the thing was virtually flawless. They had thought it out brilliantly. It was a peach. An utter beaut. Stifling considerable regret that he hadn't thought it up himself he wrote a letter devoid of platitudes in mauve ink, promising that he would do what he could to publicise the affair. He would do this not only among his colleagues, but also, he declared, with one or two well-placed poets in the country who were concerned with reputable publications and competitions and were still friends of his from the old days. He would do it, too, if only to prevent himself from coming up with a variant scheme one day and attempting to float it. Spreading the word now as noisily as possible would make that impossible. Likewise, he went straight to Dr Patience and showed the letter from Emilia to him and Miss Ogilvie, as well as his own reply, sensing that this would be a shrewd idea too.

He would never have anticipated the reaction, but the Principal Librarian was shaken to the core.

'That *poor* woman, that *poor* woman,' he kept saying, striding up and down. 'One of our true poets, the true voice of one of our own people, and what she must have suffered from such abuse. It puts wholesome Reject Letters into quite a different perspective, doesn't it? Nature, who can accomplish anything, has even designed a specially-programmed scavenger to suck the blood out of our own defenceless donors.'

Seldom had Miss Ogilvie seen him so distressed. Dr Patience actually shook his hands in the air. He told her to distribute copies of the correspondence to all staff immediately with instructions that all Librarians were to read all the poems out of moral support over the next few days. He then wrote an impulsive personal letter to Mrs Stokrotka, endorsing Mr Payle's offers and tying himself in knots, since his sense of outrage and chivalry made him talk about publishing the entire collection of poems immediately.

After a sandwich and glass of orange juice, however, he revised the text with Rosemary, and wrote out a more considered version, again by hand, and not in mauve ink either. But it would be some time before the effects of this crude villainy passed from the Principal's mind.

☞ 14 ☜

A second hiccup in the Library's tranquillity also started with a postal item. A young lady called Selena Woking wrote to the Principal Librarian to say that she was working on her PhD thesis on less well-known children's books of the twentieth century. She desired to come to the Last Resort Library and examine the collection of manuscript children's books that had, as it were, never become known at all. What interested her, she explained, were stories that had been written in imitation of or directly under the influence of a very well-known and successful book that had been, and often remained, a best-seller. It was her proposition - trite in the view of the Registrar and the two Children's Fiction Librarians – that all successful children's books – if not all successful books - engendered derivatives in this way. She was anxious to establish a distinction between self-perpetuating books of this kind (published and unpublished) and original and unconventional books (published and unpublished). In order to earn her doctorate, she would add to her analysis an evaluation of the respective roles of creativity, imitation and originality in children's books in general in the twenty-first century (as far as it would have progressed by the time she typed the final page).

So they had a meeting about it, the four of them. The request was a trifle problematic. In principle, of course, they welcomed scholarship and scholarly enquiry. Miss Woking's request, however, was tantamount to asking for free access to a very substantial part of the Library's core holdings. Asked for an off-the-cuff estimate of the number of Rejected Children's Books they held, Peregrine Constable-Barber reckoned on eight or nine thousand; Amanda said, quietly, nearer fourteen. Since she had spent several years pottering around in the stacks the Principal Librarian was more inclined to believe Amanda.

Unbound children's manuscripts – like Library manuscripts in general - were housed in Conservation-endorsed boxes, with title and author inscribed on the spine. Reject letters were usually stored with the manuscript to which they referred, loose within the boxes. This meant, as Constable-Barber pointed out, that the material was horribly vulnerable. They would need to be sure that an individual reader would act responsibly and not disrupt or disarrange the system. Or, indeed, *pinch* anything. Neither Librarian could quite visualise allowing an outsider the liberty to roam throughout the collection. Amanda, who was usually far from talkative in front of the high-ups, astounded her colleagues by pointing out that this research proposal would rapidly endow Miss Woking with a unique collection of unusual - and effectively *unused* - children's plots. As well as earning her an advanced university degree this might also be designed to set her up on a career as a highly successful children's writer.

Dr Patience was astounded. Despite his quietly nurtured Plan and the status that he accorded the Library's contents because of it, it had never occurred to him that their scribbled outlines, narratives and ideas might have an immediate monetary value. He looked at Amanda with renewed respect. This was a right-thinking girl. Amanda Bickerstaffe, an English graduate with one published children's book to her credit, had come to them after a period as a conventional children's librarian followed by the editorship of a short-lived teenage literary journal. She was now just thirty-two, and had long curly hair that was never properly under control. She was comfortably plump but always nervous in anything more than one-to-one contacts. Amanda had been a chain-smoker until she arrived at the Library, so her long fingers were always restless and intertwined when she did speak. It was her long-term plan to produce a critical catalogue of the Library's children's volumes. There was the usual *card* catalogue already, of course, as each item had been allotted a record card on accession since the very beginning, but what was written on each was usually extremely rudimentary. Amanda's catalogue was well under way by now, but even classification was a moveable feast, and no-one expected her work to be completed in the near future. Especially since Children's Books was one of the Library's most fertile areas of expansion. In addition, therefore, they would need to clarify how this young woman's intentions might actually affect Amanda's own work.

'We don't have to tell her what we've got here exactly, do we?' said Hugo. 'I mean, we can show her some sources to keep her quiet without letting on about the rest, surely.'

'Tricky,' said Peregrine. 'We are an official reference library, are we not? Can we actually *hide* stuff, Principal?'

'I think there is a beneficial distinction in a Private Library like ours between allowing people to see specific things that they ask for, and gratuitously telling them about everything we have so they can ask for it all. There is fortunately no external catalogue that this girl can consult – in advance of Amanda's great work – so there is no way she can have the *faintest* idea of what we have here. Second, to accomplish what she wishes to do, she would need to read great quantities of manuscripts more or less in full, would she not? That is very time-consuming, even for a seasoned reader. She will have to pay for accommodation in the village while she's here - she needn't know about our guest rooms, and if by chance she has heard of them Stavros can be 'decorating' them or 'removing dry rot' whenever necessary. Mrs Mowbray is not cheap and nor is the pub. If this girl is a student, she won't be able to keep that up for weeks on end. So probably our best bet is to act warm and friendly, tell her that she can certainly come and that we will sort out for her a representative selection of Reject Manuscripts - so that she will get an idea *on her own* of how impossible her plan is. I am sure Amanda can turn up some suitable stuff? I am thinking here, obviously, of (a) truly awkward handwriting, (b) really excessive length, (c) eight or

114

nine neo-Swiss-Family-Robinsons and (d) preferably a good sprinkling of books with thickly religious overtones. A week of that sort of diet should put her off for good.'

'Yes,' said the Registrar. 'Actually, there is a good lesson here, Principal, how we as a body should act when faced with this sort of tiresome approach from outside. After all, we are not a ... *lending* library soliciting *readers* – he snorted – needing to make a pretence of public service. We are a pure research institution, set on a special course beyond the understanding of ... well ... let's face it, most of the public outside.'

Again the Principal felt a thrill of appreciation at the excellence of his people. What a team! How lucky he was!

'So much so,' continued Hugo de Butler, 'that I am thinking we might draft a *Standard Operating Procedure* for repelling unwanted enquiries. Pamphlet sort of affair. Be a good time-saver if we made a breakdown of the main principles – *Keep the Buggers Out* springs to mind as general approach – with a set of techniques, written and telephonic. I always go for excessive-helpfulness that masks non-cooperation, but there are many other techniques. So, a working list of procedures, cross-referenced to relevant correspondence maybe, with space for notes. And, as you say, Principal, details of off-putting expenses that would inevitably be incurred. Then we wouldn't have to have to think the whole matter afresh whenever one of these blighters writes one of these damn letters. Not, mind you, that it isn't pleasant to be thrashing this sort of thing out together like this of a morning. What do you say, Principal?'

'I think you certainly have something there, Hugo. Perhaps you could throw some ideas together on paper and all senior staff could have a chance to add their input. It is interesting; this is the first really troublesome request of its kind to come in since I have been in charge here. I quite agree with you that if we make short work of this one it should be instructive in many ways for the future.'

So, Miss Ogilvie wrote a polite letter to say that the Last Resort Library could accommodate a week's reading visit by Miss Selena Woking in the last week of March. The Library Reading Room was open to readers (not including staff, of course, who could read anywhere all night if they wanted to, and they often did) Monday to Friday from 10.00am - 1.00pm, and from 2.00 - 4.00pm, closing completely for one hour for lunch for the benefit of the supervisory staff. Miss Ogilvie thoughtfully included a railway timetable covering the two nearest stations for visitors coming from London, the number of the costliest minicab company operating in the area, and the telephone numbers of the two fairly far out bed-and-breakfasts as well as the village pub. Miss Woking was asked as a formality to include by return a covering note from her PhD supervisor at the University, for the benefit of Archives. The wording was checked and approved by Dr Patience, who suggested with finesse that the letter should go out with a second class stamp.

No reply had come in the post by the penultimate Friday in March, and several staff members breathed a sign of relief that their unwanted guest was not to attend after all, but the Porter's bell rang sharply at five to ten the following Monday. Miss Selena Woking had arrived.

Stavros gaped wordlessly at the sight of her. Miss Woking was young and exquisitely slim, with swept up auburn hair, wearing a wrap-around fur shoulder job over a waisted black jacket and matching pencil skirt. She had high close-fitting boots and a great deal of elaborate jewellery. She had just stepped out of a little red sports car of Italian make, and she was undeniably, unforgettably, lethally beautiful.

'Can I leave the car here?' she asked the Porter, casually. Her voice gave the impression that it was slightly too heavy to speak with.

'Er – yes.' He swallowed. 'Yes, of course. I'll park it for you, Miss.'

'I've left the key in the ignition. Could you possibly take me in to the Library? I have an appointment with Mr P. Constable-Barber in two minutes.'

'It will be a pleasure, Miss Woking.'

Stavros walked beside her in silence, opening doors for her and gesturing chivalrously for her to proceed. He could detect perfume of a kind that was absolutely new to him, and it produced a great and sad longing in his otherwise philosophical and contented heart. He wished to slow down his normal pace just to prolong the experience, but his companion looked twice at her watch as she walked.

Mr Constable-Barber would be at his desk, and there was no time for Stavros to warn him. In any case, what could he possibly say?

He knocked at the door, and turned the handle.

'Good morning, Mr Constable-Barber. You have a visitor, Sir, a *reader*. Miss Selena Woking.'

☞ 15 ☜

In addition to her contribution to Dr Patience's *Booklet*, now nearing completion, Rosemary Ogilvie DSO had a gently-unfolding plan to write a history of the Last Resort Library from the inside. There were endless files and a few autobiographical notes from the first two Principals, and she had turned up an envelope or two of significant photographs and newspaper cuttings. She liked to spend odd moments in Archives, chasing up leads and clarifying names and dates. Dr Patience, had he asked to read the manuscript at any particular time, would have been gratified to see that it was the intellectual side of the Library that was her chief preoccupation. Nevertheless, as a good historian – for that is what Miss Ogilvie had long before been trained to be – she had an eye for the historic moment when it came and after it went. Thus it was that she wrote in the privacy of her 'grace and favour' flat (as Montague sometimes referred to it) that the arrival of Selena Woking marked a new and irrevocable step in the history of the Last Resort Library. She was right.

More than a handful, perhaps indeed a majority of the older Library men fell for Miss Woking on sight. In fact, as far as Miss Ogilvie could judge none of her male colleagues seemed to be entirely unaffected. In most cases, at least as far as she could tell, nothing actually *happened*, but in the end she was never sure. There were endless cubby-holes and odd corners on site if you knew where to go. And the unsupervised Woking person managed to be present within the perimeter fence for a sequence of whole days and nights. What she did know was that in the face of this new phenomenon the resources of their precious Library were suddenly defenceless, and that enthusiastic assistance was on immediate offer for the slightest whim or articulated need on the part of the charming new Reader.

A desk in the Reading Room had been made available for her before her arrival. Here she established within minutes a sort of regal headquarters. Somehow, for example, there were flowers in a vase at one corner and what appeared to be a doily for her coffee-cup. She laid out a new white notebook and a couple of sharpened pencils, and bent her shapely brow attentively over the first volume of *Swiss Family Robertson*. Within half-an-hour Mr Constable-Barber was seen by Amanda Bickerstaffe to come over for the third time and this time say to her,

'Of course, this little collection is not the really important stuff. We must have a good fourteen thousand manuscripts in our Children's Book stacks, you do realise? I think I'd better take you round so you can have a proper look, and really get an idea of what we have to offer you for your work.'

Amanda leaned against a case of Adult Fiction, feeling sick. In a flash she realised what was happening, and what certainly would happen. She would have to act at once to protect the Collection. *Student my foot*! she thought. What student could afford to dress like that? She must be a spy, on a sinister payroll. What was her game? Well, it was up to her to find out. No-one else would do it.

At lunch in the Canteen on the first day Selena was surrounded by admirers, but all she would accept was one plain yoghurt and a cup of unsweetened black tea. She was unwillingly introduced by Mr Constable-Barber to Mr Sorensen, who came in for a sandwich, and stayed longer, and Mr Ffolke Leguid, in charge of Biography and Autobiography, who was a ladies' man of international repute, and had known instinctively when she set foot in the building. Even Dr Patience, who had been told by Miss Ogilvie of Miss Woking's arrival, thought he would take a look for himself over a bowl of Sadie's green lentil soup. Ffolke and the others were still being charming to her long after 2.00 pm, and it was with considerable grace that Miss Woking looked at her watch and said that she really must be getting back to her work.

Afterwards it was never quite clear to Miss Ogilvie or Amanda Bickerstaffe who would have suggested that it was really rather silly for Miss Woking to have to leave at four, since it still got dark quite early, and she could surely stay in one of the unused guest bedrooms for the week. Equally, there was no reason why she shouldn't be allowed to come and go like the rest of the staff, since it was absolutely necessary for her to get to grips with the Children's Literature holdings for her important research. It must have been a senior member of staff. Certainly by the Tuesday evening Miss Woking was known to be browsing freely in the stacks, much to the gratification of those who worked anywhere at all near that area. The desk light was still on at her Reading Room desk and her handbag still slung over her chair after 11.00pm, a time by which the keenest Library staff were usually both off the premises and otherwise engaged.

Miss Bickerstaffe, busy about the section with lists that needed checking and ladders that needed climbing, did her utmost to keep an eye on where the spy was and what she might be up to. That very afternoon she had heard the Woking say to her boss,

'Have you ever found anything really exciting in here, Peregrine?'

only to hear him reply,

'Oh, this place is a treasure house for any child reader,'

and later, in a wondering, tell-me-all-about-it tone she asked him,

'And what are all these?'

Mr Constable-Barber's response, as she strained to hear, was revealing in more ways than one:

'Space; aliens; inter-galactic stuff. A very strong field. Lots of new plots, new galaxies, new robot languages. I love them, been working on them for years. This one, for example, stars a kind of cosmic Robin Hood with a bunch of reformed astral criminals,

robbing rich planets to feed the poor. Wonderful material. Good colour pictures too...'

'Gosh, could I have a peep?'

'My dear, be my guest...'

Amanda was giddy with rage and resentment, and, what made it worse, alone with the problem. There was nothing tangible that she could take to the Principal, and no-one else would take any notice of any word in criticism of the girl. It was desperate. It was then that she thought of Miss Ogilvie, who had been such a stalwart in dealing with the infuriating American female. Amanda grimaced. Right now she would swap the American Female for this hoyden and *embrace* her. It was late, but she would do it anyway. She would go and talk to Rosemary.

Miss Ogilvie was not in bed, but she was in her nightdress. When she heard the knock she fetched her dressing gown and went, full of curiosity, to her front door. It had been a very long time since anyone had disturbed her in her private time in the evening, unless it was a summons from Dr Patience with some specially urgent or important work. She smiled when she saw Amanda.

'I know why you're here,' she said, 'come in, my dear.'

They had cocoa in Miss Ogilvie's tiny kitchen.

'They've all got it,' said Miss Ogilvie. 'All the male librarians, I think. Your Mata Hari is a true professional. She turned all their heads in minutes. I watched her do it. It's up to you and me, my dear.'

'Thank God you are here,' said Amanda, fervently. 'But what is she after?'

'That is for you to find out,' said Miss Ogilvie. 'Madam has a *handbag*, doesn't she? Well then. Have a good look in it. Maybe there's a diary, or identity card or something. She is no student, that's for sure. I asked her specifically for a tutor letter on arrival and nothing has been forthcoming. No-one else seems to have even noticed. That young woman cannot ever have set foot in a university, can she?'

'I think she works in a *brothel*,' said Amanda. 'How can I possibly look in her bag, Rosemary? Someone might see me. Imagine that. They'd *lynch* me. I tell you, if she decided she wanted my job, I think the Con-Barb would just throw me out there and then. It would be easier to go in her room and see what is there, wouldn't it?'

'Dr Patience would protect you. Fortunately I don't think he's in love with her, and he thinks you are a very good thing. But a room probe is also a good idea,' said Miss Ogilvie. 'Perhaps we should try both prongs of the attack. I know, if we set off the fire alarm, you could hide in the stacks and come out when they had all gone outside and do the bag job. At the same time I could whip through her suitcase and stuff down the corridor and see if there is any clue. We can compare notes at the bridge half an hour afterwards. I'll bring some bread for the ducks for cover. Once they're outside they won't dare to come in until the Fire Brigade have given the all clear.'

'You'd bring the Fire Brigade here under false pretences?'

'What false pretences? That girl is a walking incendiary device and could destroy this entire library. But I'll ring the station and warn them we are having a practice, and have a word with Stavros, so when they are all outside calling the register he can keep them there for a good twenty minutes, allowing us free access. What do you think?'

'A good scheme. But if she is half as clever as she thinks she is you won't find anything except part of a PhD thesis on children's books and a lot of expensive lingerie.'

'We'll see. She didn't know that she would be staying here, did she? There must be something incriminating somewhere. KGB membership, maybe. Now, off to bed with you and dinna worry, girl.'

☞ 16 ☜

They met, as prearranged, on the bridge, arriving separately. Miss Ogilvie had remembered the bread crusts, and leaned over the parapet with her paper bag. Ducks came obediently from all directions.

'Well?' said Amanda.

'You first,' said Miss Ogilvie.

'She's on the pill,' said Amanda, darkly. 'That I *can* tell you.'

'She *is* a pill,' said Miss Ogilvie.

'Anyway, I found nothing. Her name really is Selena Woking, at least that is what is written on her driver's licence. No gun, no spy camera, no syringe. Just normal girly paraphernalia. She must have taken her precious *notebook* with her through your smoke and flames.'

'She's an actress. She works for a film company,' said Miss Ogilvie, 'a well-known British film company. They are on the hunt for a children's blockbuster, and badly need a plot with a new twist. There were three letters, or rather notes, in a large envelope zipped into the lid of her suitcase. You might like to read them?'

'You *took* them?'

'Of course not. I xeroxed them in the office at the double and put the originals back exactly as they were. Just like the old days,' she added reminiscently. 'Take a look at these.'

The first was a scrap torn out of a notebook, the second a printed receipt, and the third a typed memo:

Lena:

I think the best idea is to present yourself as a postgraduate student from some university writing up your kids book thesis, as we discussed. Get what you need from Wardrobe etc. That ludicrous library must be absolutely full of good ideas going to waste. Once in there, just see what you can find. The old farts will

be eating out of your hand in no time. Remember, we only need one bright idea for the writers to get their teeth into.
Good luck.
Geoff.

Receipt

S. W.

Cash advance enclosed, for one week's expenses and car hire &c. &c £250.00

Please keep your receipts.

J. J. O.

Accounts

Confidential
From: William Snuffield
To: Selena Woking
In re: Basic Desiderata Areas:
1. Orphan-makes-good type thing.
2. Clever child criminal
3. Some kid in particular historical context, e.g., cavemen, Bible, Third World War, French revolution or whatever? But new.
4. Baby with parent from another planet would be good
5. Good inheritance plot; switched baby/twins mix-up plot.
6. Anything else that strikes you as new and ultra commercial. You'll recognise it when you see it.

Amanda breathed out and looked at Miss Ogilvie.
'What do we do now?'
'I think I must talk with Montague. It is Wednesday morning now, and she will theoretically be here until Friday

afternoon. Mind you, we can't really expect him to throw her out bodily. He's already had to do that once, hasn't he? Gosh, *what* a time we are having. Or *maybe* …'

She fell silent as they wound their way along the path. Plan B was called for. Amanda said nothing. There was clearly an uninhibited and inventive side to Miss Ogilvie that she hadn't suspected at all. It seemed sure that she would think of something.

The Library staff, meanwhile, had returned to their posts after the fire practice. Amanda went straight into the Children's section, but no one was there. Her boss's door was open, but there was silence. She went into her own room and sat stolidly at her desk. Her notes and papers, normally a constant source of excitement and interest to her, might as well have been a pile of ashes, devoid of life. Her very work seemed to have become pointless.

Nothing happened for an hour or so. Then the phone rang in her office. It was a man, unknown to Amanda, who said that he wished to speak to Miss Woking just as soon as was possible. The voice was cold and official-sounding, and Amanda, forgetting her own grievances, promised responsibly to go and find her and get her to call back. That was fine, said the man, but in that case she would need to make a note of the number. He dictated it slowly, twice, and rang off. Amanda ran to the Reading Room and to other obvious places, but there was no sign of her quarry. Worried, she telephoned the Porter and asked him to find Miss Woking. Ten minutes later he returned her call to say that she was apparently closeted with Mr Leguid, who wanted her to look at one or two autobiographies in his room that had been written by authors whose works were now in the Children's Section. Amanda called Mr Leguid, who said regretfully that the excellent Miss Woking had just left him and gone off for a meeting with the Principal Librarian. There could be no bursting in on Dr Patience. Then she thought of Rosemary again…

'Hello there,' said Miss Woking in her most relaxed style, leisured with just a hint of post-coital intimacy, 'you wished me to call?'

'I did,' the frozen, deliberate voice told her. 'You are Selena Margaret Belle Woking, of Broadwood Avenue, London NW1?'

'Yes, that's me. Who is this please? Is this some kind of a joke?'

'Not remotely a kind of joke. My name is Commander Skelton. I am in charge of the Intellectual Property Wing of the Fraud Squad at New Scotland Yard. Your file is in front of me now. You are at present driving a red Lotus with the following registration [he spelled out the number, slowly, once]?'

'I don't know the number, for God's sake. It's on hire.'

'We know.'

'So?'

'Do you have a lawyer?'

'Of course I don't have a damn lawyer. What do you want from me? I'm just an ac-'

'Get one. Perhaps-' he paused, '*Mr Snuffield* knows a lawyer.'

'*What?*'

'Be at the following address in North-East London today by 4.00pm. *at the latest* [he dictated the address, slowly, once]. Ask for Mr Black. Third floor. We know *all about you*, Miss Woking. I suggest you make your excuses straightaway to Dr Patience, collect your few possessions and be on the road to London within twenty minutes. There are forces at play here that you cannot begin to understand, but I will tell you one small thing to help concentrate your mind: *your "PhD" is over.* Do you take my drift, Miss Woking?'

The distant measured voice was hard and relentless. Miss Woking had turned pale, and was now altogether white. 'Yes,' she whispered.

The phone disconnected.

They were in an Indian restaurant in the nearby town, Dr Patience, Rosemary, Sigurd, Hugo and Amanda, and had sampled several lagers by the time the food came. After the *pappada* (as Montague insisted the plural should be) Miss Ogilvie passed round her copies of the three incriminating letters. Hugo read them out in a variety of accents. The conversation was very lively. None of them had actually seen the deadly red car leave, but two of them had heard it.

'By the way, Mr Constable-Barber has intimated to me this afternoon that he wishes to retire,' said the Principal in the lull after the first course. 'He declares himself to be "unable to go on." I don't know why, exactly. Sigurd and I were hoping that you, dear Amanda, could see your way to taking up the position of Head of Children's Literature in the very near future. It would mean, I fear, an increase in salary, to be unworldly just for a minute...'

Amanda's day had pirouetted through an extreme of activities and emotions. It was inevitable that she should make some sort of speech. Her words were to the point and appreciated.

'Can we talk shop for a minute?' she continued, as the courses began to pile up. 'I have been reading some really horrible letters. Batches of them. It struck me that a really extensive swim through those murky waters might lead to something. It did. I think I know what they think, these people. I think I know what is going on.'

'Excellent,' said the Principal. 'Fill us in.' He patted his mouth delicately with his napkin and swigged some lager.

'Is it acceptable to mention the term "education experts" at table? Well, "experts" on children maintain the tenet that there is a *specific vocabulary level for specific age groups*. Teachers, apparently, believe this. And the book trade believes *them*. So, 8-10 year-olds can cope with one level of vocabulary, 11-12 year-olds another and so on. The stunning consequence of this perception is that any successful children's book that has merited publication must have been specifically orientated to one of these Ages of Man, and, and follow me closely here, *only utilise vocabulary that they already know.'*

'*What?*'

'Yes. They actually believe this, and promote it consistently by their actions. *Children should already know every word in a book that they might be expected to read.* None of these experts seems to have realised that children learn new vocabulary by their very encounters with new or unfamiliar words. That they get meaning from context or etymology. As when they learned to talk in the first place.'

'So all these marvellous books are turned down flat because they get the wrong reading on the "vocabulary-meter," as much as using a passive voice now and again, or favouring length in a sentence?'

'So I see it. Everything is sacrificed on this altar of *we know what's best.'*

'Well, what is to be done?'

'I would like to give a lecture to a room full of the English teachers who propagate this treacherous gospel.'

'Do you have a working title in mind?'

'Yes. *If you were a grandmother, could you suck an egg?'*

Miss Ogilvie caught Hugo's eye and winked very deliberately. This girl would do good things, they were thinking.

It was only on the drive home that Amanda remembered to ask Miss Ogilvie about the phone call.

'Oh, that was an old friend from the war. We were ... code breakers together. He was completely terrifying even then. I just called him up, gave my old password, and said that we had been infiltrated by an enemy and needed high level help with decontamination. He asked me a few pertinent questions, and that was that. It was his idea to send her with expensive legal help all the way to the house in Hackney. Simple, but effective.'

'Why, what is it, then, that address?'

'He just made it up.'

17

Despite their damage-limitation operations, the Last Resort Library was subtly altered after this episode. Several librarians became drawn into themselves, less talkative and apparently more thoughtful. No one quite understood what had happened, but subconsciously they were waiting for a word from their Leader, to make everything feel normal and secure again. Dr Patience was aware of this, but couldn't quite see his way to falling in with it, the reason being that he was not entirely sure what had changed himself.

Their innocence – or naiveté - had been tarnished, he supposed. An institution of ideals, serving unborn generations and men of all faiths and creeds had run slap-bang into a highly-developed parasite that had spotted them from afar, and attached itself to batten on them and grow fat. Not only that, their characteristic back-turning on the universal creed of monetary value in pursuit of their own ideals could no longer be quite so easily sustained. This slap in the face meant that they could never, from now on, trust outsider motives to match their own, just as they could no longer hide from themselves that part – be it a handful – of what they possessed might be or become commercially valuable.

The Registrar's unfinished *Guide to Repelling Visitors* now took on validity over and above a whimsical dislike of intrusion or interruption; it would become a manual of protection. How all this was to affect their behaviour from now on seemed, to Dr Patience, unfathomable. They could be careful, even flatly uncooperative, by all means, but what of their brief, their function, the old *Garden Centre* business?

He felt that he had really taken a body blow himself. The Christmas Evening Bonanza thing for next year was off, for certain. He was so glad that he hadn't really mentioned it yet to anyone (at least not in as many words). The possibility of inviting all those false conspirators together under their roof to be their guests filled him with horror. The idea of trying to influence them seemed footling and pathetic. They were infinitely tougher and more ruthless than he and his Librarians could ever be. His instinct now, on the contrary, was to build a moat and install a drawbridge and leave the status and nature of literature to its own devices.

He felt low. He said as much that afternoon to Ffolke Leguid, who himself was most uncharacteristically mooching about listlessly in the stacks a week after the Woking had gone. The Principal felt close to Ffolke; he was entirely stable and solid, and had been around for ever, like Rosemary. They were the two most important of his people, he often thought.

Ffolke Stratford Leguid was in fact the oldest member of the Library staff. He had read for a degree in anthropology in the late thirties, and after an undistinguished RAF war, worked throughout the fifties in very dangerous country in Africa pursuing elusive anthropological details that he had never, in fact, published. He had been protected from these dangers by a striking and rigorous moustache of the kind that is seldom seen in real life. This moustache had intimidated savage animals, hostile tribesmen and police officers with equal success, and had also proved irresistible to women of a startling range of nationalities, ages and textures. He had stomped around with the Founder on more than one bit of ground (in and out of Britain), and had been brought in by him years before to take over Biography and Autobiography. According to Miss Ogilvie's understanding, this appointment was made chiefly on the grounds that Ffolke himself had been working for years on a putative *Memoir* (reputedly entitled *With Gun and Moustache*), and should therefore be in a position to know all about such things. When the Founder had made the proposal, Ffolke had been home from Africa for some time and saddened by the lack of bi- and quadrupedal danger in his life. Why he had accepted the job puzzled everyone who

knew him (or met him subsequently), since there would be no hunting of any kind to be had within the Library grounds where he spent all his time. Perhaps he had burned out, or perhaps he had simply taken to the work, for Ffolke turned out to be as wonderful a seducer of reject biographers as he had been of women, and his years on the staff had brought in, often via a moving and grateful bequest, very substantial numbers of biographical and autobiographical manuscripts.

Ffolke was not, truth to tell, really a literary man. He was always working at his desk, surrounded by paper, but attempts by his colleagues to squeeze out of him views on, say, typology (in which they were all interested) were unsuccessful. He had never presented a theory at one of the fitful seminars in which colleagues were encouraged to keep the others up to speed on their researches. This didn't mean, however, that he operated without structure. Dr Patience knew for a fact that Ffolke nurtured a private classification system that derived from his days as a student, viewing biographers and autobiographers alike as Animistic, Fetishistic, Polytheistic or Monotheistic on the one hand, and Nomadic, Hunter-Gatherer or Urban Complex on the other. Moreover, in his own way he had achieved extensive progress with a catalogue. He always insisted on reading each autobiography in full, and, unlike all his colleagues (for whom a received text was sacred and never to be tampered with), Ffolke tended to pencil in marginalia as he read, expressing approval or disapproval, especially where individuals or events he had known himself were concerned.

Ffolke, like one or two other Librarians, had digs in a nearby hamlet, and cycled to and fro wearing his trousers tucked into long thick socks. Those who had known him for long implied that he had worked through the virgins of a hundred adjacent villages, but this probably wasn't true. The old techniques had mellowed into a gentle chivalry that made (for example) his door-opening a pleasure for any woman, and in the view of Dr Patience (who had his file) and Miss

Ogilvie (who knew a lot about the world), the tiger had grown safe and predictable. This didn't mean, however, that there hadn't been a quickening of Ffolke's systems at the sight of Miss Woking. Despite himself, he had begun to slide into the old moves, but he was only alone with her for minutes, in an open area or very briefly in his room with the door ajar, and so reluctantly he had had to let it go.

There was still, he was thinking now, some faint trace of her lingering elusively about the stacks where she had worked.

'Well, Ffolke?' said Dr Patience. 'Where do we go from here?'

'What on earth do you mean, Montague? We go on as usual, of course. Nothing has changed. We are doing the right thing here. Too big a business to be knocked off course by a combination of a hussy and a floozy. You'll see. Bolt all the doors. Few weeks, few new heavy deliveries, and we'll be back where we were. Let's have a Spring Equinox Party or something. We'll all be right as rain in no time, you'll see. Old campaigners like us. But that Selena,' he added reflectively, 'what a number ...'

The only male Librarian who was totally unaffected by recent developments was Mr Grubb, in charge of Novels, who had been away for over a month lecturing in Canada and America, and was now returned, reinvigorated and slightly over-stimulated by his experiences. He had spoken there widely about the Library and its work, with the result that several large consignments were coming by sea, donations from one or another audience member who had been moved by Mr Grubb's oratory into relieving their lofts and sheds of troublesome responsibilities. He had not visited the California library on this trip, and had certainly not gone out of his way in his talks to advertise them as a possible alternative home. The fact was that Mr Grubb had also been on the staff of the Last Resort Library for a good number of years, and had been involved when the Americans first decided to follow their example. The Founder's visionary policy sat ill when transported outside, he had always felt.

Montague had called Mr Grubb in now for debriefing, and they were talking together in his room with the door firmly closed. The Principal was wondering whether to fill Mr Grubb in about recent events, when the latter changed the subject entirely. What he had really been thinking about while he was away, he said, was *outreach*. Getting word of their work *out there*, to touch many more people than could find out about them in the old-fashioned way. Word of mouth, he said, was all well and good, but every day families who had never heard of the Last Resort Library were merrily chucking their relatives' unpublished writings into skips, or feeding them into garden bonfires. The ideal to strive for would be, he said, to upgrade public knowledge of the LRL to the point that people would remember in time, just as they swung up a sack-load or struck a match, that there was, somewhere in England, a place that would want the stuff. Sure, there had been media work over the years, but the world was changing and becoming smaller. Could they not do more, he asked, throwing his hands out eloquently, to rescue more of England's Rejected Books from everlasting perdition?

'What we want in my opinion,' said Dr Patience, 'is *more* manuscripts with *less* personal contact and *no* personal visits.'

'But you will always have to do the tea-in-your-room and the walk-round-the-stacks bit for people who cannot make up their minds,' said Mr Grubb. 'We owe it to them and you do it brilliantly.'

'That is certainly a part of my job,' admitted Dr Patience, 'it is any other blasted visitors that I want to avoid.'

'I suggest we talk over this outreach for rescue idea at the next meeting,' said Mr Grubb. 'What say I write up a discussion paper for circulation in advance?'

'Good idea. Do that, Mr. G.'

Mr Grubb's ensuing document was a disappointing blend of old Library tradition with a naive topping of slightly hysterical propaganda. His proposal came before the principal staff, who had to read the paper for unwilling discussion in Dr Patience's room.

'This term outreach,' said Ffolke airily, 'I rather think it must ultimately be an American idea, isn't it?'

'Probably,' said Mr Grubb. 'It was in the air when I was there myself. I was most struck with it.'

'A good analogy,' said Ffolke. 'You make it sound like a disease and that's what it is. It creeps into institutions via a single carrier, and spreads like poison ivy, until everybody is *reaching out* round the clock. Then they get self-conscious and feel they ought to employ a 'qualified' out-reacher to show them all how to do it properly. An Outreach *Officer*, it's called. This costs a lot of money, because professional Outreach Officer-*finders* have to be recruited to find the most fluent exponent of the cult jargon on the market. Eventually this person arrives. After re-decorating their office their immediate task is to turn the institution on its head by concluding that before their appointment nobody in that institution has ever really known what they are doing. So then in comes an expensive new *Manager*. Montague retires. I go back to Africa. Rosemary buys a seaside cottage. The whole of the Library is then entrusted to the youngest, least-qualified librarian, and off they all go, merrily REACHING OUT in every direction ever after. And the work of the collection goes hang.'

'You're against it then, Ffolke, or what?' said Montague. 'It's a little unclear.'

Ffolke grinned. It *was* an unusual sort of statement from him. Mr Grubb looked at the ground dolefully.

'I just thought it would help bring in more manuscripts,' he said.

Rosemary felt more than a twinge of sympathy with poor Grubb, and put her hand on his arm for a moment.

'Probably there are two types of outreach,' she said with her invariable directness of manner. 'One is that just alluded to so subtly by Ffolke, but he is right in his analysis. Many of my institutionalised friends have tearfully divulged the same depressing narrative to me. Here we must be on our guard. We know where we are going; we have known from the beginning, and we are not afraid of self-appraisal either, are we Montague? So we don't need that stuff. But the other kind of outreach - with a small "o" – is real. But *this*, I think, we do anyway, do we not? Judiciously, when it will be most helpful; with lectures, talks, trips here and there, and what have you. You, George, as much as anyone. And our manuscripts never stop arriving. It would only take a bit more radio or television exposure and our facilities will be stretched to their limits. My conviction is that we already have the balance right: reach out too far and, if I may put it this way, you fall out of the window.'

Sigurd smiled and Mr Grubb even laughed.

Our Rosemary, thought Dr Patience to himself for possibly the thousandth time, is worth her weight – if one might allude to such a statistic – in Gutenbergs.

☞ 18 ☜

It was April, and about time, thought the Principal Librarian, that he made a bit of an appraisal of some of his staff. Tyranny was not Dr Patience's strong suit, and he liked the liberal feeling that his people could be left unhampered to follow where their research led them. Always assuming that research was being done. It was not entirely clear to him, for example, that their Mr Payle really researched much of anything. (Not that that was necessarily anything to worry about, exactly.) But Mr Payle still made him feel, in some hard-to-define way, uncomfortable. He wasn't fully one of *us*, he decided, and possibly even, to some extent, one of *them*. But one of *whom*? Perhaps he should have a little chat with Mr Payle about what had actually been achieved over the last twelvemonth. Yes, he would do that. In a week or two.

More pressing now was Dr Boehm's *Catalogue*, both volumes of which stood reproachfully on his side table, clamouring for attention. They were now, so he had been led to understand, completely ready for publication. The novelty of this situation for the Library, which he had expressed earlier to the author, was no exaggeration. He was still faintly incredulous, but there they were. And now something had to be done. Dr Patience had, at this moment, entirely no idea who might undertake the publication. Oxford, maybe? Or one of the scholarly music houses? Hmm. As he mused over the possibilities it came to him that, realistically, he would never be able to bring himself to ring up any kind of *publisher* and make the proposal that they should publish an LRL catalogue. The only real option was to publish the thing themselves. Guenther, being only human, would want his work to be reviewed and discussed and sold. The work was such that it could attract attention in many quarters. Its appearance might lead to Library enquiries, if not visitors. Viewed from that standpoint publication was a much less desirable outcome, of course. What to do?

Miss Ogilvie put her head round the door, offering tea. He pointed at Dr Boehm's imposing volumes, and raised his eyebrows. She knew at once what he had been thinking.

'Montague, we have to publish this ourselves. That is our duty. There can be no withholding from the world a major two-volume work of scholarship of which we can all be proud. As for the consequences, I propose that we face problems when they arrive. Is this not, in fact, the moment to launch that long-awaited series *Last Resort Library Occasional Publications?*'

'Occasional might not be the term. What's the word for once a century?'

'We do it ourselves, then, boss?'

'We do, Miss O. By Jove, we *do*. Dark blue cloth. Gold lettering on the spine. The works.'

'LRLOP vol. I, parts 1-2: *The Manuscript Music Collections.* Edited by GB. Under the Overall Editorship of ...'

'That latter point is quite unnecessary.'

'Come now, Montague. Any scholarly series must have its General Editor. The over-arching mind... Ask anyone.'

It seemed to Dr Patience that he must write to Guenther Boehm without delay and set out everything clearly. He reached for his fountain pen – this was no letter to be produced on a keyboard.

> *Dear Dr Boehm* [he wrote],
> *I regret to have to write to you in what might seem to be a dampening and discouraging vein, but you will have been expecting for some time a response from me on the subject of the two-volume manuscript that you have submitted for possible publication. I together with certain colleagues have looked over your text. I and they alike judge that the subject of your not inconsiderable labours is doomed to appeal to no more than a handful of desiccated specialists, few of whom are likely to have*

the means to purchase a copy of the publication, should it in fact ever appear.

Your style varies disconcertingly between extreme taciturnity and liberal prolixity. Thus many, many pages that make up your "catalogue," are virtually unreadable to a leisured man of letters, while the "analysis" (as you put it) is in complete contrast. The lamentable number of pages alone would be sufficient to deter any but the most foolhardy commercial publisher in today's world, while the endless musical quotations that pepper your writings will require costly and fiddly type-setting to an extent that seems to us to represent the final straw.

He had carefully navigated his text to the bottom of the first page.

For these reasons [he continued] *we therefore write to you now to indicate our wholehearted intention to publish your wonderful book. We consider ourselves honoured by your offer. Our entire range of resources and expertise – such as it is – is at your disposal. We would like to invite you to come in for discussions, in which you can stipulate your wishes as to font, paper, lay-out, cover design and any additional details on which you, as Author, might have views. We are also determined to negotiate with you for the most generous financial terms that we can concoct in your favour.*

Trusting that this initial approach will meet with your approval and in anticipation of your response,
Yours, in admiration,

Montague Patience
Signaculum suum

Any editing work left undone by the impeccable Dr Boehm proved to be minimal, and so before long Montague and Rosemary found themselves taking the first steps to convert themselves into credible publishers, and to sort out the unsuspected practical matters that awaited their attention. Montague also publicly recorded his resolve that Miss Ogilvie's *The Last Resort Library: History from the Inside* (in preparation) must constitute vol. II. Production turned out to be a team job and surprising fun. Printing and binding was carried out somewhere in the Far East for a staggeringly modest fee. Thus, a mere three or four months after Dr Patience's kind letter of acceptance the patient Dan delivered a number of crates into the care of Stavros Bligh, which proved to contain some three thousand sets of Dr Boehm's *Catalogue*, duly bound in dark blue cloth with handsome gold lettering on cover and spine. With pleasing modesty Guenther signed presentation copies for all interested colleagues, and Hugo accepted a further pair to break in the newly-identified shelf in the Reading Room that was destined to groan under the Library's own future occasional publications.

Dr Patience now found himself chairing meetings at which the unfamiliar issues of book launches, review copies, publicity and a press release were discussed. Amanda insisted that such opportunities be taken seriously. Proper music journals must be approached and whatever media contacts they could muster between them must be exploited to the full.

Thus the concert reviewer for a leading Sunday newspaper came to the Library to interview Dr Boehm and only escaped several hours later burdened by pages of notes, his head buzzing with hummed and whistled themes. His article, "Staving Off Obscurity," filled three pages of the Supplement Magazine the following weekend, and included a colour photograph of Guenther holding a bassoon and a viola, Dr Patience's arm round his shoulders and a pile of bundled papers stacked around their ankles. Attendance on radio arts programmes and television chat shows parachuted Guenther into a wholly unaccustomed limelight where his eloquence and ease of manner, bolstered by an assembly of striking bow ties, won him a huge postbag that was showing no sign of dwindling. At the same time the *Catalogue*, bravely priced at around eighty pounds the two volumes, began to sell hand over fist. Readers' letters of support and appreciation came from all quarters, welcome at first, but increasingly less so, most especially the letters from musicians. Guenther's subtle and well-argued appreciation of his overlooked treasures did not fall on deaf ears. As the weeks sped by, two conductors, a dozen or so pianists, five string quartets and a whole bevy of amateur orchestras wrote to ask for copies of selected manuscript scores with an eye to innovative performance.

Dr Boehm, deep in negotiations with a prestigious London concert hall for a first series of *Ex-Catalogue* recitals, came perplexed to Dr Patience.

'My dear Guenther, what have you done? Sigurd is furious with you, you know. He says that you have undermined the very fabric of our institution, and is actually now demanding that the book be withdrawn from sale. We cannot allow publication of our collections. We are all absolutely floundering here. Speak out, man. What do we do?'

'Personally I am completely delighted with what has happened, Dr Patience. It is all that I could have wished for.'

'But you've turned the whole of my beloved Library upside down, Dr B. We are now *publishers* like everybody else. Next we'll be asked to make our adult fiction available to everybody. Mr Grubb has suggested that we institute a line in penniless-lover stories under the imprint *Bills and Moon*. The unsung song will be sung after all.'

'Dr Patience. Relax. I have a possible and dignified solution to all this. Yesterday I received a letter from a very eminent music college in London offering me a new chair in twentieth century composition this October. They have created the post for me, in fact. I am fully intending to accept it.'

'Guenther!'

'Well, my work here is done, is it not? Cataloguing the books about music can be done by any reject librarian. What

I suggest is that I should accept this position and move to the college as soon as you can release me. In addition, I should like to take the Manuscript Music Archive with me. I can begin this October.'

'*What?*'

'Yes. I propose that the whole manuscript archive be de-accessed. Half of our colleagues have always disapproved of it anyway. Now they want my blood, and if you let them they will probably burn the catalogues. This cannot be right. So I thought I should just leave and take it all with me. I can use it for teaching and study, get things performed, and promote English composers and their work like no one has ever done before. I will have access to all the musicians I want – they have a wonderful auditorium. New music. Concerts, programmes, broadcasts. Out of all those forgotten, hopeless scores. Think of it, Montague!'

Dr Patience stared at him blankly. This was impossible. He *couldn't* do it, anyway, de-accession, could he? Legally, conscientiously, in any way. He bit his fingernail.

Guenther Boehm leaned forward persuasively.

'This need have no implication for Literature, Montague. Music has always been out of kilter with your real work here. It's just the manuscript scores. I will bring their names to public attention, maybe even get some money and recognition for their families. If you allow me, I can do great things with this music, Montague.'

'Leave me, Guenther. I must meditate. You are asking me to submit to amputation. You offer no anaesthetic. And we will lose you too.'

It was too much. He was deeply affected. Dr Boehm stood up and quietly left the room.

The chief and wisest librarians were peremptorily summoned by Rosemary, and shown to chairs in the Principal's study. She closed the outer door. Sigurd could hardly wait to speak, but Dr Patience raised a very imperial hand, and sat on the edge of his desk. With the minimum words he acquainted them with Dr Boehm's proposal. There was a stony silence. The others looked at one another.

'Well, colleagues ....?'

'Speaking personally,' began Sigurd, 'this dénouement seems, quite frankly, essential. Left unattended, this whole musical ... *performance* will, quite simply, undo us completely. It cannot be countenanced. If we can get away with it legally, I would send him away with the whole lot and that's the end of it.'

'I think,' said Ffolke slowly, 'that this must be a matter for the Trustees. Not to mention the lawyers. I don't think, Montague that you should have to make this decision on your own.'

'I don't think I can. Rosemary has checked the whereabouts of the trinity. Professor Macnamara is apparently in hospital in Oxford. He is now 93. Wilford Chatterton is somewhere in Sri Lanka. And there's no answer so far from Dame Gwyneth. She's the lawyer, if any of them is. But we've already looked into the thing as far as we can. De-accession in any instance can, of course, only be lawfully permitted by a unanimous vote of all three Trustees. We are pursuing a Colombo telephone number and we're chasing Gwyneth. Rosemary and I will go to Oxford this afternoon and square Mac, if he's up to it. If he dies they will have to appoint another Trustee before we can do anything. The whole thing is bad timing. My own view, let me say, is that Guenther will do unique things with this material and that this would be the best decision in the end, if we can, in fact, do it.'

'Well, if Macnamara dies why don't they appoint old Herr Schubert as the replacement Trustee?' asked Sigurd, truculently. 'That would wrap it up. Then he could do whatever he likes with the whole Library.'

'Do we agree that we should try for this?'

Ffolke said, 'Is there no way that we could set up a separate collection, in a different building, and disassociate what is happening from the real Library?'

'Impossible. From the point of view of the outside world the message will be too confusing. We are become publishers. With a goddamned bestseller on our hands. It's unconscionable, Montague.'

'Okay. Miss Ogilvie and I will go to Oxford now and beard the ancient lion. We'll report back.'

'*Published*, you say?'

'Yes, Professor.'

'A catalogue from the Library. *Published?*'

'I know it's a shock.'

'So, what exactly is the problem, again ...?'

'Well, Sir, it's like this ...'

Professor Macnamara was like a sparrow against his pillows. His bright eye seemed, in the main, undiminished.

'As I see it, Patience, pusillanimity aside, you have developed a cancerous growth there. It has swollen and developed, distorted and unnatural. Now it is fully grown with its own demands you fear that other healthy organs might come to be infected, eh?'

'Precisely,' said the Principal Librarian gratefully.

'Then operate, man, operate! Excise the tumour. Quickly and surgically, and then cauterise. I, for one, approve your courage and vision. Do it. The Library will be all the better.'

'Professor,' said Miss Ogilvie, 'I have taken the liberty of typing up a statement for you that can be signed and dated. If you will do that we can get onto Miss Fletcher and Father Chatterton. We need you all to agree, of course.'

'Show me the thing, my dear. Quite right. Very sensible. You have your pen, Bulward...?'

Father Chatterton was at another conference of world

religions. They got him in the middle of the night. The line was awful.

'*Disposing* of the collections? *Why*, man? What *on earth* is going on?'

'No, Father. Not *all*. One section. The *music*. You see, something strange has happened...

... and Professor Macnamara has advised us to take this drastic step.'

'Oh. Macnamara agrees?'

'Absolutely. You see ...'

So that was no. 2. Father Chatterton promised to send a signed postcard with his consent by airmail.

'Hello. Gwyneth Fletcher speaking.'

The primeval headmistress. He swallowed, twice.

'Good evening, Dame Gwyneth. Montague Patience here. How are you?'

'I am well. I have recently been hearing about your best seller on the wireless. A new undertaking for the Library, I dare say?'

'Yes indeed ... It is that which is troubling me ... spoken to the others ... and the thing need go no further. The manuscript territory is clear. And it is *just* the music manuscripts. No other manuscripts at all. You see, Dame Gwyneth, Dr Boehm thinks he can at the same time help some of the families of all these neglected composers.'

He covered the mouthpiece.

'I've just remembered that Dame G. was an accomplished soprano once upon a time.'

'... and there are wonderful song cycles, operas even, which otherwise will be silent and unheard for ever. They are not, like the books, *rejected*. Just without hope, without patronage ...'

He replaced the receiver and pulled out a handkerchief.

'Phew. We've done it. She'll write a letter in the morning. The three votes. A huge phone bill, probably, but we've done it.'

He would write to Guenther before calling it a day. Congratulate him on his appointment, expressing regret that he would be leaving them, and explaining that the Trustees had jointly authorised him to release their manuscript music holdings to be presented to the College for the use and benefit of their new Professor.

> *It is with heavy spirits* [he concluded] *that I contemplate your departure, my dear Guenther. You have my true admiration and affection, and I wish you every triumph in your new, exciting and visionary future. Would that we could have accomplished this vision together.*

He laid down his pen, put the envelope in his out-tray, and went up to his rooms, weary, partly relieved, but mostly sad at heart.

Several unusual things happened when Guenther Boehm actually came to move out of the Last Resort Library. The first was that the Principal went away to Edinburgh over the focal days, declaring that he was incapable of witnessing the process of dismemberment as it played out. Then, professional movers came in to help with packing the manuscripts. Two others arrived on departure day in a perfectly excessive lorry, which had a good deal of trouble with Sir Bulward's gates and made a mess of the gravel. The loading of the music crates took surprisingly little time. The last thing up the tail ramp was Guenther himself, whom the company had undertaken to move safely too.

There was nearly a disaster as the lorry was leaving. An incoming but unanticipated heavy-duty vehicle making for the Library was forced to swerve off the road and nearly bumped into a tree. The librarians and other staff were still hanging about on the steps talking in sober groups when this second vehicle drove up. The driver was, understandably, in a bad temper. He leaned out of the window.

'Dr Berm?' he demanded. 'Delivery for a Doctor Berm.'

'He no longer works here,' said Mr Sorensen apologetically.

'Stuff that,' said the driver. 'You utterly have to be joking. I've been driving this damn thing round for hours looking –'

'No. I assure you that your information is quite correct. Dr Boehm did use to work here … some time ago, now, but no more. You've missed him, I'm afraid.'

'Look, guv'nor, I am paid to deliver this thing here, and that is what I'm going to do. I am not leaving with this load in my van. So, if you'll excuse me, me and Burton will off-load.'

Miss Ogilvie stepped forward and smiled placatingly.

'What is the delivery, can you tell us?'

'Here's the manifold. Look for yourself. It's come from Germany. Black Forest, somewhere. By sea.'

'Here we are. "Gift to Dr Boehm of the Last Resort Library, England, in acknowledgement of his great work. My father Willibald's music and his piano. The composer's music and the composer's equipment, so to say." Yes, I see. How sweet. "Four chests of music, a set of conductor's blacks, an ebony conductor's baton and a Viennese grand piano, medium sized. With candlesticks and legs." You have this piano in the boot, then?'

'There is a trussed object that might or might not be a piano among the other stuff. I haven't looked. It's all a matter of indifference to me. I can't afford to get involved with guessing the identity of a given delivery's contents. I'm neither paid to nor naturally inclined to.'

'I quite see that. Well, why don't we investigate? The piano is destined for our *Reading Room*, of course?'

She turned enquiringly to the others. Hugo nodded. McTavish rubbed his hands in delight.

'Ah, certainly, Miss Ogilvie. It should go in perfectly *as we expected*. I'll go and make sure there are no encumbrances en route.'

'If you could help us, Mr er ..., to get the piano into the correct room that would be very kind. Then if you just put the chests and other bits and pieces over here we could undertake to send them on later to Dr Boehm. That would get the whole matter off your back, wouldn't it?'

'It's all one to me what you do with it, sister. Me and Burton will get started.'

The giant bundled fowl went in sideways through the double doors reposing on a small trolley, and soon the elegant old instrument emerged from the straps and sacking. On went the dignified legs in a trice. All of a sudden, there was a grand piano in the Reading Room. It was a *baby* grand, said Rosemary defensively. A bit of rearrangement and it would look as if had always been there. Montague wouldn't even notice, she continued. No one found that claim hard to believe.

'Sign here, if you would,' said the driver.

'It will need tuning, mind,' said Burton.

They signed, and the drivers left.

☞ 19 ☜

'Incidentally, chaps, do any of you think we want a … Health and Safety survey?'

Dr Patience spoke idly in the staff canteen, toying with a sugar lump. There had been a lull in the conversation at his table while Louis fetched the coffee.

'No,' said Ffolke.

'Maybe,' said Sigurd.

'Probably,' said Rosemary.

'I had this leaflet come. These people turn up and work with you for a week, go everywhere, survey your work practices and make recommendations.'

'With a healthy bill at the end, Montague?' said Ffolke.

'Fairly hefty, yes.'

'And do we have to take any notice of what they say?'

'Oh, no, I don't think so. I don't see any reason to take any *notice*. Certainly not if it sounds inconvenient in any way. My own view would be that filing the unpublished report should be enough.'

'Enough for what?'

'Well, say anybody asks.'

'What sort of thing do they fret about?'

'Oh, fire prevention, risk assessment, use of chemicals, ladders – God knows.'

'I doubt a week would be sufficient,' said Rosemary. 'I think they might have a field day here and want overtime.'

'The only point would be to ham it up,' said Ffolke. 'Leave the big paper guillotine with the blade open with some knitting needles lying around, and tuck a rat or two under the fridges in the kitchen. Give the inspector chappies something to inspect.'

'Actually, Montague,' said Hugo, 'they set foot in here and we've had it. Fire-doors every two feet, no high shelving. No this, no that. I've heard of these people. My instinct is to bin the leaflet and carry on risking our lives as usual.'

But Dr Patience had already filled out the coupon for the free booklet, and he felt constrained to look it over when it duly arrived. "I was breathing mercury vapour for years until the *Well-in-Work* team arrived. Now my lung nearly functions like before!" read a claim on the back cover. He thumbed through the prospectus. There was something evangelical about their style – new hope for all, better life, happier workers... Rosemary wanted to know if the firm had worked with a private institution of comparable size to their own, so that they could get some idea of the consequences. She offered to look into it. Montague passed it over and gratefully put the whole thing out of his mind.

Accordingly, two of the firm's missionary team arrived at the Library one morning soon after for preliminary contract discussions with Miss Ogilvie. Earlier that same morning, however, Rosemary Ogilvie had exhibited drastic symptoms of serious internal illness and been rushed to hospital.

Stavros was, for once in his life, completely distracted. On top of everything he didn't know what to do with the visitors. He had driven Rosemary very fast to the hospital, and just got back to report to the Principal Librarian, who was all over the place. Dr Patience wanted to go out to the hospital himself, there and then, but Stavros pointed out that she would be in theatre, and the *ship would be adrift* – he must stay at his post.

Dr Patience was now sitting mournfully at his desk. He thought he might be experiencing palpitations. He went for a slug of whisky out of the drinks cabinet and sat staring out over the gardens. A future without Rosemary would be unendurable. He felt his heart through his shirt and seemed to detect an unfamiliar irregular hammering. He picked up the phone and dialled Rosemary's extension for consolation. She didn't answer. Not like Rosemary. Did she have any family? There was her sister, of course, and a niece, he remembered, in Wellingborough or somewhere. But she wouldn't die, would she? Of course not. Although according to Stavros she was doubled over in pain, white like death, drawn and unrecognizable. What the *hell* was wrong with her? And just out of the blue? If she did die they would fly a black flag from the roof for ever after. Stavros said that they had wheeled her straight into surgery. He couldn't stand to think of it. He had never acknowledged to himself the extent to which he depended on her.

He got up abruptly and went through into Miss Ogilvie's room. Her desk was immaculate as always. A neat list of commitments and items to remember. He scanned the day's entries. *Hlth & Sfty. ppl. 11.00am. For discussion.* No appointment with surgeons or angels of death. He looked at his watch. These damn healthy people must be here already. There was absolutely no way that he could face them himself. He would go to the hospital. He had to see the consultant. Make sure. He would do anything, pay anything, whatever. He wished he had married her or something. He would immediately if she promised not to die.

Mr Swan and his adjutant Mr Burroughs meanwhile were growing slightly impatient in the Reading Room. Melanie Zong, the Duty Officer for the week, had been given no steer by Stavros, who ushered the two grey-suited gentlemen politely to one of the sofas in the middle of the room, and promptly departed. She had no idea who they were, or indeed about the hospital drama that was playing out in the background. Someone would come, in due course. She kept her head down and nervously pretended to herself that they were not there

Mr Swan got up and began to explore the room. He tapped the glass of the nearest cabinet with a critical fingernail.

'No reinforcement at all. If some child rushed in here pursuing a football and collided with this pane, I wouldn't like to answer for the consequences.'

'Absolutely. The thing is a monstrous hazard. I'll make a note.'

He made several notes. The library steps – a late-eighteenth century beauty from a gentleman's library rescued years before by the Founder – was a complex of sinister dangers: rickety steps, slippery leather, dainty hand-rail. It would obviously be prone to topple over if more than two people used it simultaneously. The company catalogue happily included a range of replacement models, state of the art in red shiny metal tubing that would permit an elephant to retrieve a book from any high shelf with impunity. Mr Burrows uncapped his pen again.

'Oh dear, oh dear,' said Mr Swan. He pointed eloquently to the wiring behind the photocopier. Mr Burrows nodded. 'The whole place is a death trap,' he whispered. 'And this, so to speak, is their Front-of-House. They've let us in here, quite unashamedly. Lord knows what we will find *behind the scenes.*'

'Indeed. I dread, positively dread, the laboratories. Probably arsenic in among the tea-bags.'

They shuddered together in anticipation.

'Not to worry, gentlemen,' said the smart-looking consultant briskly in the hall. 'We've sorted out your Rosemary. Burst appendix is all. We've opened her up, washed her out. Good as new. She'll be back on the tennis court in no time. Although she must have had a lot of pain in the run up to this explosion. Silly girl, not to tell anyone.'

Montague swayed against the wall.

'I say, are you all right, Sir? Perhaps you'd better come with me.'

He reached for his walkie-talkie.

The Principal Librarian had certainly picked a good place for an eye-catching display of cardiac crisis. Stavros reported the details later that evening, explaining that Montague and Rosemary were now in adjacent beds. He had some kind of tube in his arm, but Rosemary had been heard to ask if he had any letters to dictate. It seemed likely, concluded Stavros, that "we would both be pulling through." He would be offering a visiting run with grapes and stuff for those interested. Ffolke flatly refused to go anywhere near any hospital and Sigurd was anyway committed to friends of his wife for dinner, so all those who really wanted to go managed to squeeze in. Surprisingly Pomfret Payle was determined to join the party. He had found something that very afternoon which he was certain would cheer Dr Patience up.

'And Rosemary, too, surely?' said Mr Richardson.

'Er, well …'

Miss Ogilvie was sitting up in a pink bed jacket reading when they arrived, evidently enjoying the change from Library routine. Dr Patience was apparently unconscious or asleep, but he woke up the minute Stavros manipulated the cork out of the champagne bottle under his coat and started handing round shot glasses. There actually *were* grapes, too, somehow. Everybody was kissing Rosemary and fussing over her. Mr Payle sat tentatively on the edge of Montague's bed holding his glass. He had never seen his chief in pyjamas before.

'Dr P., I've sneaked out a letter that I absolutely have to show you. I found it in a box of old typed poems this morning. It's an old deposit, possibly not even registered.'

'Pomfret! Don't tell Hugo.'

'I wasn't going to. Anyway, I smuggled it out to show you. Have a look.'

He handed over the faded sheets. They were fixed together with a rusty paper clip.

> *Corfu*
> *July, '27.*
> *Reggie,*
> *I am working on a new thing, to be called I think Klymaks. It begins:-*

Blued with narcissus sheen
the swollen capsuled membranes
shuttered her smudged eyes.
Below a newspaper billowed
by the rat-pecked bricks,
and time,
thudding somewhere quietly
marked her again with its persistent
subtle crease.

There will be more. It's going to be good. The reason is there is a protruding Castilian maid here, over-warm in invariable black, with a slight moustache. She will do it for cigarettes. So the American tells me. He's probably right. He has a slight moustache too. Perhaps it's contagious.

The proprietor here, her boss, an ample, charismatic man of sixty or more, makes his own flies for fishing. There are many on display under the glass counter in the vestibule, and guests always admire them while he is checking their passports and so on. He picks one out when he needs it. We polished off a bottle of some brandy or other under the trees last night. I instructed him he should invent a different bait that would catch mosquitoes. He told me very confidentially that the secret of tying effective flies was to incorporate a woman's pubic hair in the knot. I derided him. I condemned him for disseminating an old wives' tail, but he didn't understand. He went indoors and brought me the proof. He has a little silver box with supplies in. He opened the lid just for a moment. There were several distinct colours in the collection. They looked convincing in as far as one could tell from a distance. I pretended to believe him, and asked him as a fisherman myself whether he came across them lying about, as it were, or whether they were kind donations, or what?

He explained that he made a practice of procuring them himself for stock whenever the opportunity arose. The best technique, he said, refilling our glasses with what was left, was to time it to the moment of most intense gratification; donors seldom noticed, and, as he put it, you could snaffle two or three at once. I thought of asking him if he needed contributions, but the box as far as I could tell was comfortably full. I'm sure the maid was already represented anyway.

So you see Reginald I am still upright and fighting. Send me some poems for God's sake. Better still, bring them out here yourself. There is drink here as well as hair coursing in abundance and the moonlight after both is unspeakable.

As ever, my dear boy,
TSE.

'TSE?' said Dr Patience. '*TSE?* Hello? I may be fuzzy today, but those initials ring a bell. What's the date again? *Could* it be Thomas Stearns?'

'Well, of course, Dr P., that was my idea too. I dashed home to find the *Works*, and went frantically through them to see if there was any echo of any of these working couplets that might have resurfaced later.'

'And?'

'Nothing.'

'But this would be a whole new angle on the man, Pomfret. The informality of his outlook on life and love, and his *hail-fellow-poet-well-met* relationship with this Reggie. Any ideas on who that might be? Not a nickname for old Ezra, maybe?'

'Well, you see –'

'It doesn't conform to my view of Eliot at all, I must say. Something there to make the critical establishment sit up a bit. TSE with his trousers down, so to speak...'

'I was thinking on identical lines, Principal. But when I got back to my study I found an envelope under the chair, and it must have belonged with this letter. The rust here from the clip makes it certain. The letter and its envelope must have got separated from one another. This proved that the recipient, who clearly wrote all the other horrible poetry in the box, rejoiced under the name of Reginald L. Haigh. However, the name of the sender was written out on the back of the envelope. TSE turns out to stand for someone called T. Selwyn Eastman. So much for my discovery!'

Dr Patience began to giggle. Rosemary looked over warningly; it was clear that she had already resumed her previous role. She had slightly pink cheeks, and didn't really seem entirely intimidating, but Dr Patience pulled himself together.

'We'll keep this as a secret between us, then?' said Mr Payle.

'More or less. But I absolutely have to show it to Rosemary, later. She will appreciate it as much as we. She probably knew him. Eliot's Corfu Years!'

There was some commotion outside in the corridor. Someone on a stretcher was being wheeled through from Accident and Emergency. Or rather, two people. Both were prostrate and heavily bandaged. They would all have to be a bit quieter, they were told.

'What's all this, Sister?'

'They've come in from that weird Library place up the road. We had to send an ambulance. Two men got involved in a nasty accident. Some packing cases fell on them in a basement, the girl said.

'So, what exactly can you tell us, Miss Zong?' asked the Inspector. He had driven out to the Library with a Constable. He had never set foot in the place before, and was more than curious.

'Well,' said Melanie, 'they were sitting over here, waiting, while I was working. I heard them conversing quietly, but I didn't really pay any attention. I assumed that Dr Patience or Miss Ogilvie would be coming soon, you see. I didn't hear about what happened to Miss Ogilvie until later. I was on duty early and was hard at work on my paper.'

She pointed to a pile of manuscript.

'Go on.'

'I sensed them walking about – I think they were admiring the furniture. I was embedded in a really awkward footnote, and when I came up for air they were no longer there.'

'What did you do then?'

'I half got out of my seat, and then decided that they must have gone back into the vestibule, or perhaps even gone outside for a smoke. One of them smelt pungently of pipe tobacco.'

'You had personally made that observation, Miss Zong?'

'Yes. It was unmistakable. It reminded me of my grandfather, you see. I suppose I must have put it all together subconsciously.'

'Possibly. And what happened next?'

'Well, I then noticed that one of the side doors of the Reading Room was open. Normally it shouldn't be. It leads to a rather dusty staircase, one of the routes to the central basement. I went to investigate. I was just thinking that the footprints were rather fresh-looking when I heard a lot of noise from below.'

'And what did you do then?'

'Well, I went down the stairs, of course. There are about

ten steps, and the passage goes to left and right at the bottom. The noise was coming from a storeroom off to the left. I looked in through the door. There were two pairs of trousered legs poking out from under a load of wooden packing cases. One pair was twitching. I knew no one would hear if I called from there, so I tried to pull the crates off one by one. The two gentlemen who had waited in the Reading Room were to be found underneath the pile, and rather badly hurt. They were solid wooden sea crates with metal trim, you see. They had been stacked up against the side wall in the room, which was otherwise empty.'

'And then?'

'Well, I had to go for help. One of them was virtually unconscious, and they both looked in a bad way. I dashed back upstairs and phoned for an ambulance, and then went looking for help. I found the two binder boys, Jimmie and Richard, who were playing football outside, and Amanda came down too. But we didn't do much until the ambulance came.'

'And what do you think happened to them?'

'I can only assume that they came prying downstairs, and wandered into this room, and tried to extract the very bottom crate from the pile for some elusive reason, and brought the whole thing down on their heads. I have no idea what could have motivated their behaviour. The crates were perfectly stable, and have never fallen down before.'

'Well, these men exhibit signs of bodily damage scarcely commensurate with what one expects in a conventional library. That is why we were asked to come and ... take a look. You see, Miss, there are four people now in that hospital ward who earlier in the day at one time or another were all *in this library*. According to the matron, whole weeks go by without a single specimen of a librarian being in the hospital at all. That could be what we in the Force call "suggestive," if you follow my mental?'

The Constable nodded.

'Arguably. But this sort of investigation is not what I have been trained for, Inspector,' replied Miss Zong politely.

'What I mean is,' pursued the Inspector, 'that these injuries are more the sort of thing that one associates with the phrases "deliberate assault," "grievous bodily harm" or "attempted murder."'

'Indeed.'

'Yes. I gather that these men were professional *inspectors*, so to speak?'

The Constable grinned.

'Actually, Inspector, I am not sure who they were.'

'They were *inspectors*. They were here to take a look at your library for misdemeanours in the field of health and … *safety*. There they certainly got more than they bargained for. But my point is, could it be that they got too intrusive or impertinent somewhere and one or two of the more *manly* librarians – he smiled at Melanie to show that he did not include her among the likely suspects – might have decided to teach two nosy parkers a bit of a lesson? Huh?'

He folded his arms and looked at her steadily. A good point well made, he seemed to say. The Constable folded his arms too.

'It's quite probable, Inspector. Librarians do tend as a species to be characterised by untrammelled savagery. A reader studying here not so long ago, for example, inadvertently knocked one of our books off the edge of the reading desk onto the floor with his elbow. Beefy, the Duty Officer, took him outside and had at him with a baseball bat. It's the only way. Faced with unreasoning brutality, you see, readers fall into line. I would imagine these inspectors probably asked some thoughtless question. The poetry librarians or someone will have marched them down here and beaten them up, finishing off the job with our old packing-case-trick. If they come round, show them photographs of the more virile staff and they'll probably identify the culprits instantly. Unless the trauma runs too deep.'

'This attitude is not helpful, Miss Zong. My years as a policeman teach me (a) that all in this library is not what it seems, and (b) that the twinges in my psychology make me think of suspicious behaviour. Are you in fact able to put my mind at rest, or do I need to telephone Forensics?'

'Inspector. I think you need not feel anxious as to (a). All libraries have this effect on sensitive people's psychologies. It's all the ideas lying around. As to (b), why not wait until these poor men have recovered and ask them *what they were doing* under our packing cases in the basement? I can assure you that your own curiosity on that score can hardly rival our own ...'

Hugo meanwhile found himself, he supposed, in charge, since rather to his secret pleasure there was no sign of Sigurd anywhere. He offered the Inspector a glass of sherry in Montague's study just to see if he would really say "not when I'm on duty, Sir," but to his surprise the officer accepted with alacrity, and even the Constable had a bottled water, fizzy. They sat together on Montague's handsome furniture.

'It's an odd case,' said the Inspector. He was visibly enjoying his sherry. No one could say Montague was careless in such matters. '*Several* cases, you mean, Sir,' said the Constable unwisely.

Hugo smiled absently. It had suddenly occurred to him to wonder whether the victims would consider that they had a possible claim against them. The proposition was sufficiently absurd to be just conceivable. Boxes in a private basement should probably be labelled *Do not peer underneath; only loosely stacked*, on the off-chance that some outsider might one day come down and test the issue for themselves. Never mind that the twerps were effectively trespassing. He would keep quiet for the moment, though. Whatever happened, Montague and Rosemary must not be disturbed. He stiffened his back. Such was the price of responsibility. He gestured hospitably at the bottle.

Stavros and Millie, meanwhile, were watching television together. This happened seldom nowadays, as Stavros was usually working on his Norwegian lessons, and Millie always had a thousand more interesting things to do than watch television, but the stresses of the day had been such that both wanted to flop in unison. Now that Dr Patience and Miss Ogilvie were out of danger the stress could begin to recede. Stavros had certainly been through it. In fact, they had both frightened the life out of him. He heaved himself out of their deep sofa and went off to look for a really good bottle. He wanted to drink the health of the P and O line, as he thought of it, and it would need to be something really good. Millie read the signs and fetched two of their best glasses out of the cabinet.

'Their healths,' proposed Stavros gravely.

'Their healths,' seconded Millie.

Montague lay pensively awake, but breathing as if deep asleep. The night light at the sister's desk reminded him fleetingly of being ill as a child. There would be no actual marrying Rosemary, of course. She never had been married, for one thing – as far as he knew, although there had been lots of practice and rehearsals, as she had put it – but she wouldn't want to be starting the experiment now. And, anyway, Montague felt that his own total of three wives was already enough for a man in his position. There had been no children, but that had never worried him. Psychologically he now felt himself an old bachelor who to all intents and purposes had always been a bachelor.

Montague had emerged with little from his various marriages beyond a quantity of useful money. The whole saga of episodes seemed very remote, nowadays. His first wife, a fellow student all those years ago, had committed suicide as a young woman for reasons neither he nor anyone else had understood, then or since. The second, an Australian singer with ample funds behind her, had died after three months of galloping cancer, while the third, turning up under impulsive and colourful circumstances very much later, turned out in the end still to be married to someone else, and later spent time thinking that over as a convicted bigamist.

These accumulated experiences seemed to him, when he did think about them, wide enough and sufficient in themselves. He now faced the future with total equanimity. Dr Patience combined the affable solidity of a senior churchman with a deep-seated adherence to unswerving atheism. It was a pleasure for him to debate theological issues with a good opponent, preferably one with a dog collar, but few of his colleagues had parallel interests and the professional clerics of his acquaintance knew better. His colleagues' religious lives, like their personal lives, could always remain, by an unspoken Library principle, remarkably private. In the same way, few of his colleagues knew about his parade of former wives. Ffolke Leguid had actually managed to meet two of them, but never alluded to that privilege. Rosemary knew all about all of them, for there was very little that he had not talked to her about over the years. He valued Rosemary, now that he had been forced to face the thing, more than all of his wives put together. This was a pleasing insight too. He would do nothing to upset their seasoned equilibrium. She was recuperating splendidly. He smiled to himself in the darkness. Life was a strange affair ...

Shortly after dawn, Montague woke feeling on top of the world. The nurse had looked at his chart and remarked that he had managed the smallest possible kind of heart attack, and in fact he was now feeling in better shape than he had for years. He thought he might recommend a really small seizure to all his friends. He patted his drip affectionately. Whatever the stuff was, it was a good vintage. What is more, the others had obviously told Rosemary that his heart had given out through worry about her. He fingered his unshaven chin thoughtfully and smiled appreciatively at her in the adjoining bed. She was wearing her spectacles and rapidly filling in a crossword.

The workings of hospital life appealed to him, too. The danger, the small band of dedicated workers, the crucial issues of life and death. It was akin, in some measure, to their experiences in the Library. He toyed with the conceit in his mind. Montague wondered, as he lay there, whether any of the medical staff had ever committed their experiences to paper. He must ask them, encourage them. He dozed off again.

'You have a visitor, Dr Patience,' said the ward orderly. It was mid-morning.

Sigurd came in, holding his briefcase. There were no further grapes, Dr Patience noticed. Astonishingly he was wearing a roll-necked sweater and corduroys.

'Good morning Principal, Miss Ogilvie. We are, I trust, on the mend?'

'We are, the two of us.'

Rosemary waved distractedly. She was now deep in another book.

'Any idea how long they will keep you here? Hugo and I are on top of everything, of course, but the Library is not the same without you both.'

'Worry not. We'll be back installed at Headquarters in a few days. Rosemary will soon be running the gymnastic class as usual. I'm not allowed to lift anything, so someone else will have to re-stack the packing cases.'

'Actually, Principal, we've burnt them. Once the Flying Squad had finger-printed them all for their files. We thought it best.'

'They've gone home now, the Boris Karloffs. One had a broken jaw, and the other still wouldn't talk to anybody. We never actually did find out what they were after.'

'A mouse, apparently. They saw one, and were absolutely determined to prove to you that we have a rodent problem in the basement. They market a specially effective and costly kind of humane trap, I gather, and wanted you to invest.'

'Yes, well, their application is admirable.'

'All this can wait, but apparently they will not be suing. Hugo made a couple of firm telephone calls.'

'Good man. Any other news?'

'You have an edifice of mail waiting for you. Hugo opened anything that looked pressing or official. It seemed right to us, Principal?'

'Yes, indeed, Sigurd. You have done well. Anything else meaty?'

'Well, *inter alia*, you have an invitation from the secretary of the Publisher's Association to address them on the subject of the work of the Library.'

'Sacred Erasmus! Hear that, Rosemary? They are coming to *us*, the Philistines! I can preach in their temple before the idol. When is it?'

'A few weeks off. It's over a Thursday and Friday. They are offering you forty minutes and an honorarium.'

'Well. This is indeed gratifying, Sigurd. I shall get something down on paper immediately while I'm stranded here. Forty minutes, eh? They'll never recover.'

Miss Ogilvie looked up.

'Steady, Montague. Calmly. No dangerous excitement over there, please.'

'And it's years since I received an honorarium. We'll share it out. With everybody.'

☞ 21 ☜

The publishers, followed by assorted publishers' assistants, shuffled out of the University's draughty lecture theatre into the coffee queue in the vestibule. One or two were hungry churchgoers, glad to have reached the termination of a sermon, but most were laughing, and there was certainly a buzz of conversation. Those who procured coffee filed out through the French windows onto the patio. Many drew cigars; from a distance the group of plump men and their attentive seconds appeared like duelists, wreathed in triumphant smoke, choosing their next opponent from the contenders.

Dr Patience was still at the speaker's podium, a small knot of younger people crowded anxiously round him. He looked down benevolently at their heads. He had done well, he knew, in his address. It had come out perfectly, patrician without pomposity, visionary without hysteria. He had certainly held them, or most of them. And without a glimpse at the scribbled plan that had remained unneeded in his waistcoat pocket. The question was, what would be the outcome?

When it came to it no force could have prevented Dr Patience from accepting the invitation to speak. Ffolke and the others had seen it as a brave move – head in the lion's maw and so on – but the collapse of his earlier schemes had not changed his conviction that there was work to be done out there, and this was certainly a choice opportunity.

The challenge had been to slide imperceptibly from matters of theory and principle to the gist of his speech, which was how to get hold of the piles of unwanted literature that he knew littered the costly premises of all those who sat before him. He reasoning was this: when an individual submitted a manuscript for consideration to a publisher, everyone knew that it must be accompanied by a stamped addressed envelope with sufficient stamps that the manuscript, unread or rejected,

could be returned to the author at no cost to the publisher beyond a weightlifter to manoeuvre the dejected sacks to the post office. From this, Dr Patience had reasoned that, in many cases, for a variety of reasons, a good proportion of the great unwashed world of would-be authors probably failed to include this essential.

What, therefore, happened to these manuscripts?

This question had been on his mind intermittently for years, and indeed he had even inquired of one or two people who ought to know, but they had each said quickly that they didn't know at all. Probably, therefore, they knew jolly well. Probably, also, the real truth was awkward. Everyone knew that publishers great and small were beleaguered every day by unsolicited manuscripts. The word "mountains" was usually heard in the context. Dr Patience suspected bonfires or shredding parties. Storage was crippling – they all knew that. So, was obliteration their customary answer?

If so, what he wanted to propose was, could they, at this fateful moment, not turn to the LRL? Might not he and his colleagues be able to step in with a beneficial service? Unbidden the words *"Lebensraum"* and "graphic cleaning" came into his mind. He pushed them away. He then thought of *dung beetles*. He shook his head. Not a helpful analogy either. Must concentrate.

'But it's all trash, Montague!' called a voice from the back of the room.

'Not all of it!' cried another.

'You'd go under,' came a further remark. 'You'd drown, man. We'd have to maintain a special fleet of lorries. You'd be backfilling coalmines. After five years you'd despair.'

'Well,' said Dr Patience, 'I am only wondering –'

'Another thing. Some of these lunatics believe in saturation bombing. They send their damn manuscripts to each of us, sometimes more than one. I could name them now. Reggy D. Blood, for example.'

There were groans, and cries of 'No!' and 'Mercy!' from adjacent rows.

'See what I mean? You'd have to build a Reggy D. Blood wing – the complete works, five hundred versions of each.'

There was an unmistakable noise of retching from a nearby seat.

'Believe me, Monty, you'd be begging us for paraffin.'

Dr Patience was imperturbable.

'Remember, however, dear colleagues, our primary responsibility at the Library is Literature. Not tulip manuals. Bicycle maintenance. Histories of boxing…'

'Hey, that's a good idea,' shouted someone.

There was laughter, but not hostile, he thought. A heavy-set, grizzly man that Montague remembered from some unsatisfactory meeting somewhere years before lumbered to his feet and peered up at him, holding up one hand. Everyone waited, but no remark was forthcoming. Eventually the fellow sat down again. A clear-thinking and highly successful publisher stood up then.

'The real problem here, Dr Patience, is *copyright*. These dreadful constructions still belong to people, and, as Stanford says, they are seldom unique copies. So if manuscripts went out of the fiery furnace (if that is what other publishers do – I admit nothing) from us to you, you would have no idea about the subsequent possible history of the duplicates. And you couldn't get *clearance* from the authors, could you, as I suppose you normally do? Legally, I mean. I can't see a way round that.'

'But do you not warn people that you will destroy abandoned manuscripts, like suitcases at Heathrow? Or do you just make the decision after a set period of time? Is there, do you think, any future in – let's say for a moment that you read something that is really good but you won't publish it –'

Laughter.

'Well look, hold on, you know the "this is great but not for us" letter –'

More laughter.

Steady, Montague, he told himself. He remembered Rosemary's urgent voice, concerned as they faced one another last night over the garden table, a bottle of good wine between them:

1. Don't criticise them or antagonise them

2. Don't mention what it is that we really care about

3. Don't quote rejection letters

*4. DON'T MENTION THE REJECTION
   LETTER COMPETITION*

Where do I go? The hell, what can we lose?

'Look, let me ask you all something. You know this circular?

Thank you for sending us your book, which we have all read carefully. We all found it highly original, absorbing, funny, entertaining and excellently written and we adored the illustrations.

However, I am afraid we feel unable to take it for our list at this time.

We would always be happy to look at another manuscript in the future.

Is this letter ever *true*? I mean, don't you ever find that you are holding something that you know is *good*, real *literature*, but that the ... market just won't support it?'

There was silence. People were looking at one another.

'It's *that* that I am looking for. It's that stuff that I want to rescue from perdition. Those voices.'

He waited.

'As for the copyright problem, what we would do is open a Special Collection. We might call it *Publishers' Detritus*. With a modern database it could be checked against later incoming manuscripts from more ... conventional sources. And, we won't infringe copyright. We aren't aiming to *publish* anything. We just want to rescue manuscripts ... for the ... future. For unborn researchers. Even Bloody Reggy.'

The small joke brought relaxation. There was more laughter, and people were talking.

'So look, *think* about it. Maybe, once in a while, there will be an obvious case. We will always be interested. Also, there is one other thing. We are looking for a couple of new staff for the Library. English graduates, perhaps. Good readers …'

'Yes. Me!' A girl at the back with red hair had jumped up and was waving her arms excitedly. Two others followed her example. 'Over here!'

'Well, it looks as if we might make at least one or two new acquisitions with your help.'

He smiled benevolently out over the auditorium, and raised his hands to draw to an elegant close. There was spontaneous and real-sounding applause. He bowed, graciously.

Dr Patience hankered painfully after a cigar himself. He was still talking to the red-haired girl, and decided to skip the rest of the morning's lectures. He felt exhilarated and exhausted in equal measure. There were three people who declared themselves interested in his job offer, but the other two had gone back in to hear a report on recent investments in British publishing, which was enough to exclude them as candidates in his mind. The girl, Pamela Worthing, was charming, and seemed really keen. It was quite true, they needed some new blood, and he was thinking as he spoke that perhaps, if there were to be any feedback or co-operation from the profession, they could appoint her as a sort of liaison person with publishers. Could one really use the term "Detritus Curator," he wondered.

'Tell me, Pamela,' he said, 'do you happen to keep a diary?'
She smiled.
'Ah-*hah*,' she said.
Dr Patience laughed. He could, he thought, invite her to come to the Library for a day to meet the major staff, stay for lunch, and get some measure of the work that they

were all up to. At the same time the others, or at least the significant others, could take a peek at *her*. (One benefit of life in an institution such as theirs was that appointments could be made without advertisement or public competition, although the arrangement had had its drawbacks in the past.) Pamela would acquit herself well, he thought, interested but not pushy, keen but not aggressive. She was now telling him that she played several wind instruments in a jazz band, and confessed to a fondness for mathematics as recreation. She had slightly downy cheeks, plump forearms, beautiful hands and she radiated competence.

When it came to it, however, Pamela was treated with noticeable reserve by some of the staff. Their reluctance, Montague finally twigged, must be an inheritance from the Woking experience. His colleagues obviously assumed that he was sweet on her, and wanted her to join the Library staff for personal reasons. How to dispel such a fatuous illusion? Quite aside from her ludicrous youth, she wasn't remotely attractive to him physically and never would have been. He tested the idea detachedly. No, there wasn't an element of that factor involved. He liked her and thought she would do a good job if they employed her. That was all. He had a delicate word with Rosemary. Rosemary remarked that the girl, although scarcely beauteous, seemed a natural fit in their idiosyncratic world, which was perhaps hard on her but good for them. So it was concluded: they would write and offer her the job. If he was correct, the other thing would blow over once she had started work, Rosemary added.

Pamela would thus become the Diary Librarian, under the supervision of Ffolke Leguid, with an additional responsibility to develop accessions presented by willing publishers. Any incoming literature of the latter category would be given a P.W. number (Publishers' Waste, that is, not to be confused with the P.W.D. numbers used for the diary donation), on the understanding that waste items could be returned either to the author or any publisher who might subsequently undertake to bring out the work. Pamela had to work out a month's notice, and it was agreed that she would join the Library Staff in about six weeks time, in what, calculated Montague, feeling creaky, would be already another January.

☞ 22 ☜

Life in the Last Resort Library over the subsequent few months was, in comparison with recent upheavals, more or less peaceable. Dr Patience brought his *Booklet* to a *very* advanced state of completion, but was now wrestling with the final dilemma. Should Dr Boehm's old contribution be included as it was, or should it be redrafted to keep up with recent developments? If the latter, who was to do the job? Editorial problems, he muttered.

Rosemary, knowing he was so preoccupied, knocked apologetically.

'Montague, I think you need to see this letter from Mr Dibsey personally...'

He began to skim, but then read carefully.

> "... *It must be thirteen years ago now,*" continued the letter, "*that you will have received my late stepfather's manuscript Memoirs. My mother has recently passed away, and I found your receipt among her effects, here enclosed. I knew he was writing it, of course, although I never actually saw the manuscript myself. The thing is, I want to read it. In fact, I would like it back. I wish to publish it, you see. My neighbour is a book publisher, you see, specializing in do-it-yourself manuals, and he says ...*"

Dr Patience lowered the letter and sighed. *Bugger*, he thought.

> "... *he was always good to me. I won't even mind if it makes a loss. I can subsidize it with some moneys I have come into in other ways. So, could you send it back to me, please? As soon as possible. I shall naturally be happy to reimburse you for the postage.*"

This problem was something that Dr Patience had long dreaded at the back of his mind. The *please-send-it-back* problem. What museums called 'restitution.' As far as he knew it had never cropped up before. The contract of donation was, of course, both clear and permanently binding. Much legal time had been lavished on the wording: *I hereby declare* – he knew it by heart. So much for Mr Dibsey. A man whose very handwriting was irritating.

> *Dear Sir* [he wrote],
> *With regard to your recent letter, you are of course perfectly welcome to come to the Library to look at your stepfather's manuscript. But I must advise you that the terms under which that manuscript was made over to our possession by your late mother mean that we are quite unable to relinquish it to you personally. Our legal department long ago took great pains to secure all eventualities, and we are, in fact, forbidden by our very statutes to release or de-accession any of the Last Resort Library's holdings.*
> *Trusting that you will now understand our position, to which no exception can be made,*
> *I remain,*
> *Your obedient servant,*
>
> > *C. M. Patience, PhD., etc.*
> > *Principal Librarian*

The reply was as instantaneous as was compatible with the abilities of the post office:

> *Some obedient servant!*
> *This is intolerable. My mother was probably semi-senile when she made that gesture. I want my step-father's book back, and fast. Otherwise I shall ask my solicitor to get on to you. I am a tax-payer, you know.*
> > *Dennis B. Dibsey*

Faced with this trumpeting declaration of war Dr Patience summoned Ffolke, who read casually through the correspondence and shrugged:

'Tell the blighter to go to hell. Agreements is agreements. He can't muster a worm-eaten crutch, let alone a leg to stand on.'

'I know, but frankly, Ffolke, do we need this kind of trouble? Look, just *find* the pesky thing, can't you? Let's see what it's like.'

'We are not backing down in the face of bluster and violence,' retorted Ffolke, 'even if he is a "tax-payer." Tell him once and for all it's *no go*. You return one thing like that and manuscripts will be going out the door every five minutes. All sorts of descendants will change their minds. Anyway, if I am to find these *Memoirs*, we need more information to go on.'

Bibliographical details were likewise not slow in coming through:

I am glad you are seeing reason.

'No we aren't,' said Dr Patience aloud.

My lamented stepfather was called E. Smith. His manuscript was bound in black. Strangely, there was nothing written on the outside, as I remember my mother telling me. It was hand-written, in a code specially invented by him.

'Jesus,' said Ffolke, 'Am I not due some annual leave, Montague? A completely unmarked binding, and all those years ago. Lucky it's such a distinctive name.'

'Forget leave. Do we have other volumes in *code*, do you know?' said Dr Patience.

'Dunno. Hewg used to be interested in that stuff. Technically, of course, I don't think any of them have actually been rejected *qua* codes. They have usually come in with other items.'

'Yes,' confirmed Hugo, on the phone. 'We do have a few. I've been thinking of writing them up. I deciphered three or four once upon a time – simple substitutions, of course, but amusing.'

'Were any of them ever really tried out on publishers?'

'One, certainly. I remember a couple of letters to the effect that the book-buying public were to be challenged to crack the code for themselves.'

'Hmm. Compelling marketing device.'

'Keep me posted, man, 'said Hugo, disconnecting.

'It's not clear to me why we took this single volume at all.'

'It is clearly some early idea of Bulward's. Are you looking for an excuse to avoid confrontation, Montague?'

'Does it sound like it?'

'It sure does. In my view, we have to man the battlements. There can be no special cases, Montague. This Dibsey fellow has sent us back the receipt, hasn't he? Can't we just sit tight and deny everything?'

'He probably made a copy.'

'True. But in *code* ... ,' said Ffolke, reflectively. 'I *say*, Monty, I have just had an idea ...'

A day or two later he rang Dr Patience to report that he had managed to locate the Smith volume. It had the black, non-inscribed cover that had been mentioned, and he was sending it down to Conservation to pass it for ultimate release to a Reader.

> *Dear Mr Dibsey,*
> *I write to notify you that your late stepfather's manuscript is now available for you to consult in our Reading Room. We will be open to Readers on the following dates ... Note that we have stocktaking coming up, which means an unusually restricted number of possibilities ... Kindly let us know ...*

'I am coming on Tuesday,' said Mr Dibsey, trying out Dr Patience's telephone number. He had a petulant voice, a little too high, a little too strident, a little too much all round.

Reader Dibsey drove up on Tuesday mid-morning in a muddy and rust-punctured estate car. Stavros classed him at once as a weasel, small bristly moustache and more than the hint of a squint. He looked back weasily at Stavros through the window and wound down the glass. Stavros pretended to consult a piece of paper.

'Mr D. B. Dibsey?'

'Quite so. Where do I set up?'

'Set up?'

'My tent.'

He gestured towards the rear of his motor.

'I will be reading here. For some days to come. Ask Dr Patience.'

'Dr Patience is not available, I'm afraid. Can I see your camping permit?'

'Don't be absurd. You have acres of land here. Where can I install myself please?'

Stavros considered.

'I'll need to check that, Sir, I'm afraid. I'll show you possibilities in due course, if, in fact, you will prove to be over-nighting, as it were.'

Mr Dibsey was most put out to discover in this off-hand way that he wouldn't be meeting the Principal Librarian. The interview that followed with the secretary woman had not gone well at all, either.

'Dr Patience has asked me to welcome you on his behalf, said Miss Ogilvie, articulating very clearly. 'He has been suddenly called away on important business. Yes, Mr Dibsey, we are up to speed on your case. Our legal people have confirmed that we are not in a position to accede to your initial wishes as you have outlined them. We understand that you would like to see the book itself while you are here?'

'I intend to *read* it, Madam. Not only that, I shall wish to order a photocopy of it.'

'Ah, there again, there are problems, Mr Dibsey. Copyright laws mean that we are only ever in a position to photocopy *sections* of a given work, not a complete work. Also, I have some idea that there was talk the other day that the machine is out of toner. But I suggest that you pop down to the Reading Room and have a look at the original for now.'

'My solicitor has given me advice. He says there can be no objection to my copying out the entire book by hand if you refuse me a photocopy.'

'You are of course at liberty to do that. But I should mention that all copying work must be done in pencil. Bottles of ink are not allowed in the Reading Room.'

'And then publishing my ancestor's work from that.'

'Ah, no, Mr Dibsey. Publishing is, as Dr Patience will have explained to you, not an option for you. The content of the manuscript is our property now.'

'Well, you can't stop me hand-copying, can you?'

'We wouldn't wish to, Mr Dibsey, but it will be a lengthy job.'

'I am here to stay as long as it takes, Madam. No effort will be spared. I have my tent.'

'Indeed. You aren't thinking of putting it up near the Library, are you?'

'Of course. You've got plenty of space.'

'So we do. But there is a bye-law about … travellers and people regarding temporary accommodation within sight of the house. It will have to be out in the woods, I suspect. You've brought water? And there are frightful fire regulations. Many of our trees have standing orders, you know.'

'I have my small paraffin stove.'

'Sounds a trifle inflammatory. The grounds here are sometimes patrolled at night by burly ex-policemen who know their responsibilities and entitlements. We wouldn't want you to find yourself humiliatingly bundled off in the small hours, would we…?'

'Gum boots are not permitted in the building, Sir,' said Stavros.

Mr Dibsey padded irritably in his socks through the double doors, oblivious to the contemplative tranquillity of the Last Resort Library's pride and joy. He was shown to a slightly rickety table by the wall, which Dr Patience always wanted to throw away, on which reposed a black-covered volume with plain cover and plain spine. He struggled eagerly out of his coat. He had his own notebook with him, of course, several biros and a fountain pen, but certainly no pencil. He would have to borrow one. Who for Heaven's sake ever wrote in pencil nowadays...?

He sat down and opened the cover. There was a small inked inscription on the flyleaf, up near the top right-hand corner: *E.S. his boke.* Mr Dibsey smiled. Typical of his pernickety, scholarly stepfather. He rubbed his hands in anticipation and turned to Chapter 1. The page was empty. As, indeed, was the following page. A steady inspection disclosed that the entire book, from cover to cover, was similarly empty.

Mr Dibsey pushed back his chair and banged his fist on the table. Hard. Then he began shouting the word "Hey!" in a provocative and repetitive manner.

The Duty Librarian, who happened to be Mr Richardson of Non-Fiction, stepped over quietly and spoke mildly and blandly, as to a sick child.

'Come, Sir, this is not behaviour for a library, is it now? Scholars in adjacent work-places are concentrating, cherishing their peace of mind. These "Heys!" do nothing to help anyone. What, in fact, is troubling you?'

'You people are trying to make a fool out of me, and I will not cooperate. I shall demand an enquiry. I shall definitely go to the newspapers.'

'You seem upset.'

'Do I? There is NOTHING in this book, man. I have come to reclaim my inheritance, and after a very good deal of non-committal evasion by your superiors they produce *this*, and pass it off as my stepfather's reminiscences. This is not it.

No one wrote in it. No one *ever* wrote in it. It's EMPTY!'

'Let's have a look, shall we?'

Mr Dibsey looked at him with pointed hatred.

Oswald Richardson turned the pages carefully, and eyed them one by one.

'You need turn over no new leaves,' shouted Mr Dibsey, beside himself. 'They are all virgin as the whitest snow. I demand proof that this absurdity is my stepfather's book. Do you hear?'

'Let's just have a further peep here, shall we? Flyleaf inscription in black ink, Waterman pen I should judge, written by a right-handed –'

' – well, yes, he was right-handed, that is true –'

' – man in late middle age, heavily built, probable smoker…'

'Well, yes, he was, but –'

' "E. S. his boke" – quaint. That fits all right, then? He was a Mr. E. Smith, you told Dr Patience?'

'For god's *sake*, man, are you seriously –'

'Step by step, Mr Dibsey, step by step. Let's have a dicky at the case mark. Should be inside the back cover. And here indeed we are: 1963.4.12,1. This means that this volume entered the building here on December 4th, 1963, and there was nothing else with it, because we haven't any further 1963.4.12 materials. It would have been our Founder who accepted the volume from Mrs – er – Smith at that time.'

'I demand proof that this thing is the actual book written by my stepfather and given by my mother to your confounded founder. What are you telling me? Someone dropped the book on the floor and the letters all fell out and blew away? Look me in the eyes and tell me that you expect me to accept this empty book.'

It wasn't clear which eye he should look at, but Mr Richardson did his best.

'Well, I wasn't here then myself so I couldn't say what

might have happened. The Principal asked us to look out your father's manuscript from the Reserve Stacks, and so we did.'

'Is there a *catalogue* in this insane place where I can see for myself what was recorded about this book when it arrived in 1963? You know, like you find in *real* libraries.'

'We have only registration slips from that period, as a rule. The Founder used to write the details of a given accession on a slip of paper or an index card.'

'Well I would like to see the index card for this book, please.'

'Certainly, Sir. If you would like to take a seat again with the volume I'll go and see if I can find it for you. I may be a while.'

'Oh, don't put yourself out. I can be relishing another episode of the Emperor's New Memoirs while you're away.'

Mr Richardson was gone for a little over an hour. When he returned he found Mr Dibsey sitting on a desk in the corridor with his stockinged feet on a chair, drawing pictures of bodies hanging from gallows. He snorted derisively at the sight of the librarian waving a strip of slightly smeared grey paper.

'Here we are, Sir. Bit of a hunt. Sorry to keep you waiting. Let me read it out.'

'I can read on my own.'

He scanned the typewritten flimsy closely:

```
One volume, in ms. 80pp.
Personal recollections (untitled)  [in code].
Bound in black buckram; untitled.
Received as don.tion from author's relict, Mrs V.
Smith, of Leatherhead, Surrey
[see corr. s.v.]. PSO.
Reg: 1963-4-12,1.
Section: Autobiography
```

'What does PSO mean?'

'*Papers signed off.* Everything in legal order. Our usual procedure.'

'Why is "in code" in brackets like that?'

'To me, Sir, it would indicate that that is what the Founder was told by the donor at the time of the donation. He took it to be as described and never saw any reason subsequently to alter that description.'

'So let me get this straight. My mother gave His Lordship an empty book, saying, one, that it was full of interesting unpublished memoirs, and two, that it was in code. Your chap accepts it gracefully as such and catalogues it accordingly, wilfully ignoring, or possibly worse still, *not even noticing* that it was just a book of unused pages. And you lot persevere with the identical charade today, despite the evidence of your own faculties. Are all the other books here empty too?' He waved his arms in several directions.

'I think the explanation for your mother's donation and our acceptance of it is provided by the additional note on the *back* of the catalogue slip that you are holding, Sir.'

The additional note read:

[apparently in invisible ink]

Mr Dibsey held the book awkwardly up to the light and squinted desperately to make out traces of lemon juice or some other secret device.

'Careful, Sir, with our book,' said Mr Richardson.

'*You* look. Up under the *lamp*. Can you see anything?'

'Just paper fibre, Sir, for now. It must be a very subtle technique.'

'Bring a kettle. We hold it in the steam and it will come up like magic.'

'No food and drink in the Reading Room, I fear, Sir, let alone a kettle. Conservation would be drenching us with chemical foam in seconds. No dice, I'm afraid.'

Stavros came in at that point.

'Where are we with our tent, Mr Dibsey? Do we need to go off and look for a plot?'

'I should think you'd be utterly wasting your time. You've all lost the plot completely. None of you in this building would recognize a plot if it poked you in the eye.'

He walked out.

'It worked like a dream, then, one might say?' said Ffolke to Mr Richardson. They were taking tea together with Rosemary in high good humour. 'Bit of luck my finding that unused book. Actually, there's a whole pile of virgin stationery like that from the old days still in the basement, I discovered, as well as some vintage typewriters. Might come in useful again.'

'The catalogue slip was beautiful, Ffolke. Really nice touch.'

'Jot the main modus op. points down on paper for Montague. He'll be back on Thursday, and happy to draw a line under this one. He will also, I think, be amused.'

Dr Patience had certainly chuckled appreciatively over Mr Richardson's report, more than relieved that this was the end of the business. Good work all round. Hugo, he noted, had promised Ffolke that he would have a serious go at deciphering Smith's original volume. It seemed the very least one could do.

Montague's heart sank, therefore, when another envelope addressed in Mr Dibsey's hand arrived on his desk two days later. He sighed, and slit open the envelope.

A plain sheet of white paper floated out. Nothing at all was written on either side. Dr Patience laughed all over again, and then, almost instinctively, held it up to the light, just to make sure. There *was* something there. He narrowed his eyes against the morning sunshine. With perseverance he could just make it out ...

☞ 23 ☜

The painted *Music Library* sign made by Guenther had long been taken down, and Stavros was now trying to draw out the words *Diary Library* with a stencil on the back. It was much more difficult than he expected to get the letters neat. The earlier plan to install the diaries in Ffolke's small storeroom had been abandoned in the light of Guenther's departure. The main music library would need relatively little adjusting, and it was light and pleasant. It was just a matter of adjusting the shelves, but that was not so straightforward, as Wendy Twirl had discovered. She was officially Junior Librarian's Assistant, seldom to be seen, and usually charged with the uninteresting jobs that no one could put off any longer. She stood in dreadful awe of Ffolke Leguid, who had personally asked her to help him with the first diary consignment before Pamela arrived, and she was determined to do everything brilliantly. Wendy's survey of the first diary suitcase suggested an average of about six or eight inches, but Mr Wriothesley said doggedly over the telephone that he had specimens varying in height between one inch and a foot, and he refused despite a lifetime's experience to be drawn on what might represent the "average crucial proportions" of the "average" diary. He wasn't much more helpful even when they went down to see him to collect the next major consignment.

Dr Patience was in a slightly distracted frame of mind as he stood in the doorway to inspect his new Diary facility. It was rather less than one-eighth occupied, but Guenther's denuded shelves looked a lot less forlorn already.

'We've sorted them out,' said Wendy, in a rush. 'The diaries that we've got so far. We thought we'd try them out on the new shelves, now they are dry. They do look rather lovely. For a normal librarian it's a bit like being in a large doll's-house, though. Like Alice. And it raises an interesting problem. How we *arrange* them.'

'*Arrangement* is not a challenge to disconcert a professional librarian, surely, young Wendy?'

'Well, Dr Patience, one would naturally go by author, I know, but a good number of these diaries have no name in the front. And according to Mr Wriothesley, hundreds of his other diaries are anonymous. So we thought we'd do it chronologically by starting year. That way we can incorporate the *Anons* where they belong.'

'That seems far from revolutionary.'

'True, Dr Patience. But we will have to move them all up when new ones arrive.'

'So you will. Sort of musical diaries.'

'Mr Leguid says we should have got Dr Boehm to provide us with a signature tune. Mr Leguid said he wanted to arrange the diaries by *size* and *colour*. But I talked him out of it.'

'Good for you. And you have got the catalogue under way already?'

'Yes, Sir. Would you like to see it?'

All in order there, then, and the Diary Project seemed to have blended smoothly into the working of the Library without further complications. Even Sigurd, inspecting a few small volumes later that afternoon, remarked how interesting they were. He would talk with Ffolke about the staffing implications. Young Wendy was sweet and anxious, but he wanted to steer the project on to firm intellectual territory, and gushes were no good. It would need Pamela to take over Wriothesley's vision, incorporate it properly and push it forward. But they ought to be able to find more interesting work for Wendy. He moved off and went down to the canteen for a glass of tea. He wanted to re-read a disturbing letter that had arrived in a parcel that morning:

Dear Dr Patience,

You don't know me but I happen to be acquainted with a niece of your Miss Ogilvie, and she has told me all about your unusual library. I am therefore sending you now the manuscript of my book. It is a unique copy. I have tried to become a writer of children's books. The rejection letters are also included in the orange file. I did destroy some of my first go-away letters, but after a while I decided to keep them. I used to read them over every New Year's Day. Not long ago I was glad to get my manuscript into the hands of one of the best-known children's book commissioning agents. Eventually I received a short note from her, containing the worst rejection expression I have ever heard as its main point. This was the expression:

I really do not understand at all why you have even written this book.

Well, a few days later I decided to go and see this person myself, and explain personally why I have written this book. Her name is Melody Ricketts. The address was a silver and glass building in central London, new but unstable-looking. I went up to floor 81 and went down the corridor to reception and asked to see Melody Ricketts. She was not there, I was told. We had this conversation:

'When will she be back?'

'She won't.'

'Er, why?'

'She's gone.'

'When?'

'Recently. She's er - disappeared.'

'I see. Would you like to read a manuscript?'

'Er, well … (pause) What category?'

'Children's Fiction.'

'Ah, you need our Miss Ricketts.'

'Yes, I know that. That is why I asked for her. Can I see her?'

'She's gone.'

'Does she have a successor?'

'No, I don't think so.'

'Can I apply?'

'Well, I suppose anyone can apply. When it is advertised. It hasn't been advertised yet, as she is only freshly disappeared. Are you in the business then?'

'Well, it's the subject of my children's book. It's about a girl who believes that the perfect story exists somewhere and has never been submitted to a publisher because the author cannot bear the idea that it might fall into the hands of the best children's editor in the world who would then refuse it with a crushing rejection. So she decides that she must become that famous editor herself to make sure that never happens. She has a long and uphill struggle in the course of which she has to reject out of hand all sorts of wonderful stories so that her professional colleagues applaud her acumen and her promotion is guaranteed. And as this goes on over the years her true nature gets more and more suppressed. Her fame and authority in market judgement become unrivalled. And then, one day, the perfect story comes in. It is typed rather poorly on cheap paper. There are corrections by hand. But she knows after reading the first page that this is it, the magical perfect story. But by this time she has supped so extensively with the devil - relying only on a mustard spoon with a broken handle - that her heart is now blackened by jealousy, and she rejects it, with the harshest author-repellent she can muster:

I really do not understand at all why

you have even written this book.

*And after she has posted the letter, she just ...
disappears. And no-one at work ever finds out
what happens to her. And the name of the rejected
book was* The Caravan of Light and Fruit. *And
this is how it began.*

Chapter One

*The Caravan wound its way across the arid
stoniness, leaving behind the last nodding palms
at the edge of the village. The stoniness made no
difference, no difference at all. Soon there might
even be ice, or perpetual night; who knew? There
was no point in guessing. The wood of the caravan
creaked a little. And apart from the intermittent
rhythmical creaks there was a great silence...'*

The letter went no further, and was unsigned. The parcel
also contained the manuscript itself. It had been written out
by hand in little gold letters on coloured paper. Montague
held it in his hands and turned it over and over. The book
had been bound in some unidentifiable material, and the title
carefully lettered on the spine: *The Caravan of Light and
Fruit.* He opened the book at Chapter 1: *The Caravan
wound its way ...*

Dr Patience sat fixedly at the table holding the golden
manuscript in his safe and experienced hands, staring
and staring almost beyond rescue into the remotest, least
identifiable distance ...

☜ 24 ☞

It was now early spring. Walks in the grounds were a
delight. Within the buildings, however, people were worried.
All the Library's shelves, cupboards and basements (apart
from one or two damp ones) were full up. Certain recent
arrivals, some quite bulky, had not even been unpacked, as they
could not be properly housed. Something had to be done, said
everybody. So Sigurd even confessed to an outside colleague:
the problem of Library storage was no longer containable. In
addition, the labs needed extending and refitting, the high-
ups were toying with plans to recruit new staff, and there were
other ideas in the air.

Rosemary, for example, had started a campaign – mostly
kept to herself – to bring in proper computers. Rosemary
was now of an age when, in a different walk of life, she
might perhaps have thought of leaving her post to join her
widowed sister in Clacton-on-Sea. Not Miss Ogilvie. Her
place was in the Last Resort Library. Certain old friends
in quite different walks of life had long initiated her into
undreamed-of innovations in what Montague disparagingly
called "intelligence machines." She had accordingly been well
on top of the advantages that the computer could bring to
any library long before any of her colleagues, who merely saw
them as comfy word-processors where you could make typing
mistakes as often as you liked, or hated them altogether.

With these pressing and wide-ranging needs in mind Dr
Patience had just pulled off the most timely and generous
donations. It was a pretty sickly business, toadying to a rich
old woman with a terminal and wasting disease and a tempting
trunk full of her father's scholarly writings, but he had done
it. Normally the Principal Librarian was gentlemanly in the
extreme in such matters, but circumstances had merited a
full-scale campaign.

Eventually the call came from the solicitor; Mrs Sophia Hayden (née Stevenson) had died in her Southampton hospice, and would be buried in a small churchyard in Sutherland the following Tuesday. In accordance with her will, the solicitor was instructed to report that a substantial quantity of unpublished papers in the hand of her late father, Captain Samuel N. Stevenson, would soon be on its way in assorted trunks to the Last Resort Library, in care of Dr C. M. Patience. It would be accompanied by a banker's cheque for a figure involving seven highly-comforting digits and a life-size bronze sculpture of the said Captain Stevenson, executed in or around 1934 by an unknown but supposedly promising sculptor. Dr Patience lowered the phone with a whoop, and knocked back a really colossal vintage scotch - after pouring an identical one for Miss Ogilvie. Following that he wrote elegantly - with her assistance, in reply to the solicitor. He stated that he would be attending the funeral in person on Tuesday, that part of the money would go at once into building new Librarian accommodation and facilities, and, as was now urgent, additional, high-standard manuscript storage. The new arrangements, he promised, would include a Stevenson Room, in which the bust would be exhibited in an alcove, or the closest they could get to an alcove.

The journey from the Last Resort Library to the stony churchyard in the north of Scotland might have proved the end of Dr Patience, had Miss Ogilvie not decided (i) that she would go with him, and (ii) that Stavros must drive them. They would overnight in a bed-and-breakfast somewhere, and arrive comfortably on time. Mr Richardson (unhelpfully nicknamed the "Everything-Else Librarian") produced a fine three-volume rejected *Tours of Scotland Guide with Special Attention to Historical Local Churches [Illustrated]*, which they spread out gleefully on the floor to locate the church in question. And there it actually was, with a short appreciative paragraph about some noteworthy internal architectural feature, remarkable in that the whole church appeared from the description to be about six foot square. They decided that they would all dress in classic mourning for the occasion, and send profuse flowers to boot. One point seven five million quid *was*, as Dr Patience pointed out with the lucidity and perception for which he was well-known, one point seven five million quid.

Three sea-chests arrived at the Library together with a gigantic crate while they were still away. Millie rang the Duty Librarian, who recognised what they must be and called in Mr Richardson, the man responsible for any incoming material to which the word scholarly could be applied. Mr Richardson, a slim and dapper man who normally felt himself at something of a disadvantage among the literary Librarians, made heavy weather of trundling the trunks, one by one, on Stavros' uncooperative trolley, although after one look the crate stayed exactly where it was. The captain's trunks were plastered with 1920s travel labels and similar trophies, and altogether seemed full of promise as he faced them, wheezing slightly, lined up on his carpet. Undoing the fossilised straps was tough work too, and then he found that they were all securely padlocked and key-less. There was nothing to be done about that until Stavros the tool-king returned. He might as well have left the damn things in the Lodge, he realised, falling weakly into his armchair.

Not long after an unusual commotion was to be heard from the direction of the front hall and he stood up in alarm: stately silence usually prevailed in the Last Resort Library as in other libraries. A sight for the Archives camera met his eye. The Principal Librarian in crinkled evening dress, arm in arm with his Secretary in an extraordinary set of operatic widow's weeds, was dancing across the black and white flagstones that lined the entrance hall. They nearly collided with the wobbly *Recent Acquisitions* case in which spectacular new material was sometimes put on exhibition to encourage staff and the occasional undecided visitor.

'It is so *good* to be *home*,' said Dr Patience. 'Where are you all? Ring the fire bell. Let's have a damn party.'

Stavros came in then with a case of champagne on his trolley. He was in very sober black tie and tails from the waist up, but below was wearing jeans and tennis shoes. Responsible for most of the driving, his wedding trousers had proved too tight for safe work at the wheel. They had come more or less direct from the funeral, said Rosemary. It had been colder and wetter during the outdoor service and simple burial than seemed mortally possible. The Library contingent, with their absurd quantity of flowers, were the only three outside mourners. The local parson, faced with this unlooked-for attendance, had felt impelled to give of his best, both in the wee chapel, and outside in the tiny, crowded, stone-walled graveyard. Mrs Hayden's shiny black coffin which had preceded them up motorways and country lanes seemed shockingly wasteful; the cost of the ebony alone could have re-roofed the whole building in copper, fitted central heating and added computer terminals to every pew, reckoned the Principal Librarian. Water streamed over them as they stood like penguins in the mud. Finally, their eccentric benefactress was laid to rest in her austere location. They stood the parson a first-rate lunch in the pub, invested in bottles and thermoses, and turned the car flat out for home. They had shared the driving, sneezing and dozing intermittently. And here they were.

The Captain's open chests were stuffed to the brim with sheets, note-books and packages of slightly mouldy-smelling paper. These turned out to record closely-written arguments based on archaeology, ancient inscriptions, mythology, assorted early symbols and a dozen other disciplines to support the proposition that the Aryan strain was the most important achievement in the history of the universe.

Mr Richardson squatted by the first container, turning over the pages, dipping in here and there with an increasing feeling

of distaste coupled with wonder at the sheer quantity of work involved. There was no indication, he thought, that any of the drafts and re-writes had ever culminated in a finished manuscript, or indeed that anything in those much-travelled trunks had ever been *rejected* as such. He sat back reflectively on his haunches. Their Library was not in the business of housing what were just unpublished private jottings and scribbles; the entire premise was that a history of determined submission and humiliating trade rejection was essential. Perhaps, he thought, the Principal Librarian, not having seen the archive for himself, might not have realised that these manic and unpleasant papers technically had no business in the LRL at all. Bringing up such a technical point at this stage, though, might seem ill-judged. The famous *cheque* had been well banked. What to do?

There was one particular section under Oswald Richardson's care where Miscellaneous Rejected Obscenity (pornographic, racist and religious) was customarily stored. It was all down in the basement, and deliberately rather out of the way. It wasn't a large section, since families who came upon such writings after the passing of their author usually hastened to destroy them utterly, and in fact the present Principal was always anxious to increase their holdings of such literature. Yes, that was the solution. A dark corner of his Basement B12. Under suitable wraps, for the next century or so. Good idea.

He was summoned back minutes later to the front hall, however. The statue had been un-crated but was still swathed in sacking, and the Principal felt that Mr Richardson should be in on the unveiling as a reward for the tiresome job of recording the details of the paper acquisition. The sculpture was a surprise. It was life-size, as promised, but very much a full figure rather than a bust as they had all assumed, and unusual in that the Captain was depicted as stark naked and Aryan to the hilt. It was a good deal more than any normal alcove could be expected to accommodate, and did not induce unambiguous signs of respect in its new company. It was not long before all staff who were at work that day were drawn magnetically to the front hall, where they seemed happy to stay and participate in the celebrations.

Later discussion about what to do with the statue, carefully minuted in full, made up one of the most enjoyable staff meetings in the Library's history. Miss Ogilvie proposed that the Captain should be installed in the middle of the wash-basin area of the Ladies Restrooms under a grand chandelier, which they could purchase specially out of the money. Sigurd was anxious for clarity over what had been promised to Mrs Hayden's Solicitor. Once Montague's letter was retrieved and read out Miss Ogilvie was quick to argue that the whole Ladies facility, being in every sense staff accommodation, should be rebuilt from scratch, incorporating a special man-sized alcove, and then the whole affair could for ever after be called the Stevenson Room. For a while this forceful proposition seemed to be gaining ground. Mr Richardson was then asked to report very quickly on what a first overview of the manuscripts had thrown up. The installation of a Stevenson Room to house the nation's holdings of literary racism leered over by a brass-bound sea captain certainly had an appeal about it, but there was no way the statue was going down to the basement, and the obscenities were never coming upstairs. Stavros and the other technicians, chiefly Walter Denham, who was the bulkiest, were consulted on the spot; descent was deemed out of the question. Mr Bristow pointed out that there were no other members of the Captain's family alive, and the solicitor chappie was hardly likely to come down on a tour of inspection from Edinburgh and ask to see the confounded thing, so he thought the statue should be set up somewhere in the grounds, out of sight of the Library unlike the other edifice, where nature, and specifically jackdaws, could get to work on it. Sigurd conceded that in all probability he was right, but wills were wills, and promises were promises, and you never knew, and nothing should be done that could ever imperil their right to hold on to the Captain's money, as transmitted by his daughter. The Principal Librarian rather favoured a location for the statue by the lift, à la commissaire; whereupon Melanie Zong, Mr Grubb's Assistant, broke her invariable reticence at public meetings to propose that the Captain could be re-clothed in his original sea-going uniform. This suggestion met with a round of boisterous applause. Mr Grubb then calmed everything down by declaring that he had hundreds of sea stories available, and that Mr Richardson undoubtedly had endless technical manuals about ships and navigation, and surely Ffolke dozing over there could weigh in with uncounted naval reminiscences? What about a Marine Rejects room, named after the captain, with him on duty in the corner. If they couldn't get his trousers on at least they could provide him with a telescope. Mr Payle thought this ingenious, but was reluctant to fiddle about with existing categories. There were problems enough, but if they started plucking books at random and re-housing them in new groups, where would they be? It would be equally rational, he finished up, to put all manuscripts by authors *named* Stevenson into one room...

☞ 25 ☜

More seriously, of course, they would now have to put the Captain's gold to its proper use. Less than all of the sum, if they were lucky, but definitely not *more*. This little matter was something that Montague, with all the recent flurry and charging about, had not even begun to think through. Fellow directors or heads of large institutions of his acquaintance were fully accustomed to submitting proposals for huge monetary support, and knew to a T how to fill in the forms, furnishing fluent estimates and detailed breakdowns as well as convincing-looking architectural plans and models.

(In fact, for some of his peers this sort of activity took up the bulk of the working year, what with the provisional stages, preliminary stages, finished proposal and recovery afterwards from disappointment, a sequence that could be difficult to sandwich non-intrusively between proper stretches of annual leave.)

Montague as Principal Librarian had a great deal of money arrive on his humble collection plate with none of these conventional add-ons. The cheque, once everyone on the staff had seen it up close and been allowed to fondle it, was deposited suavely over the bank counter in town by him as if it were nothing out of the ordinary at all.

Now that the immediate delirium had faded, daunting considerations began to make themselves felt. Luncheon later that week at his club with several seasoned campaigners left Montague feeling green and insecure at their manifest superiority in market-place experience. Offhand remarks that began 'Of course you will already have made sure of …' as well as allusions to blithely disregarded matters such as *insurance, planning permission* and *financial responsibility* made him uneasy over his coffee and brandy, and a lot more so when he mused over them alone on the train back. He resolved to discuss the matter openly with his henchmen as soon as possible. This was a time for henchmen if ever there was one.

As he should have anticipated, Sigurd and Rosemary proved as stalwart as ever. Their innovative concept was to decide in a simple way what they actually *wanted*, and only *then* bring in professional help to achieve it. Rosemary's chief point was that the Library's work must be allowed to progress uninterruptedly throughout, and that neither donors nor other visitors (with the usual exceptions, of course) should be put off by mud and cement mixers. Sigurd's proposal was to leave the hotch-potch of buildings that represented their life and home *entirely alone*, and undertake a completely new construction somewhere at the rear. This would be out of sight, and they could all turn their backs on it during the work. It would include up-to-date paper storage – for the *Stevenson Facility* – on which they would consult the experts - and a range of new staff offices and whatever else they fancied. The new wing could be connected by some umbilical brick and plaster outdoor tunnel to part of the main complex, allowing staff trolleying documents to travel safely between them under inclement conditions. The advantage of this sort of scheme was - since they had masses of land – that come the future, when everything became filled up all over again, they could do the same and tack on another extra building limb. The immediate Library site was backed on by extensive open grassy areas before the foothills. It is not, Sigurd pointed out confidently, as if they could possibly run into trouble about *planning permission* or *heritage*. Montague swallowed. And anyway, Sigurd would deal with all that stuff when the time came.

Dr Patience thought with a pang of Sir Bulward's simple sketches, now flattened and mounted in an archive Album. Envelope backs were the right level for him too. God, he had never had such a terrifying feeling of looming responsibility. Practical complexities admixed with money complexities were just not his forte. He would acknowledge that criticism to anyone... He looked helplessly at them both. If Montague *wished*, Sigurd was steadily continuing, he and Rosemary could always rough out some sort of amateur plans for discussion *themselves*. He had done technical drawing at school, and still had his slide rule somewhere, he believed. Montague stretched across the table and silently grasped his Deputy's hand in both of his own. Rosemary laughed, and waltzed over to the drinks cabinet. Dr Patience leaned back in his chair like an altogether different librarian and felt the tension seeping down, down, down out of the soles of his shoes.

'Something comic happened earlier at the club,' he said. 'I was down in the snug talking with a couple of rare book dealers I know, in one of those very comfortable armchairs. One of them had been saving for me an expletive-bedecked manuscript essay by Hazlitt that had been turned down by the editor of some contemporary periodical. He wanted thousands for it. What is more, he was completely incapable of grasping that we would need assurance that it was never published later by someone else! They just do not take the point. I declined it, of course. But then we fell to discussing the ludicrous but universal weakness among collectors for first editions. They were both completely silenced when I remarked airily that the *true and highest connoisseur* can only be satisfied by *pre*-edition volumes ...'

In due course, hooting and grinding, the column of liberators made their way up the drive to the sight of secretaries and other staff waving in welcome from the open windows. Battle-scarred lorries, cud-chewing cement mixers, catering caravans and skip loaders ground to a halt round the back, disgorging an army of men with impressive clipboards or colourful hard-hats. Operation-room bungalows and lavatories appeared as if from nowhere. There was soon mud and scaffolding everywhere.

Library staff came to understand at first hand the three torture systems conventional on building sites: *vibration* (drilling, hammering etc.); *noise* (concrete mixing, swearing etc.), and *dust* (a special type designed to penetrate through sealed polythene sheeting etc.). All, so to speak, acquired gum boots of their own. Nevertheless, it was fun at lunch-time to watch what was going on, and the kitchen girls did a roaring trade out of a back window. Dr Sorensen was in his element, armed with a clip-board of his own, chairing many high-level progress meetings behind closed doors with harrassed-looking men with briefcases.

In sum, library life proceeded as uninterruptedly as anyone could have wished, and they had never had to turn away offers or donations, as Miss Ogilvie had feared. The employees of the Last Resort Library were still loyal and buoyant when Dame Gwyneth, Father Chatterton and the new Trustee, Guenther Boehm, came on their tour of inspection, about two years later. Guenther had put on a bit of weight, they all noticed, and had rather less hair.

By the Trustees' arrival the new storage quarters were in a once-only state of limbo, in that they were *ready* and *spotless* and *empty*; they would never qualify for this description again. Sadie and Prue pulled out all the stops for luncheon. Three slightly comatose Trustees selected Wellingtons from the Library assortment and were conducted on an extensive and energetic tour by Montague, supported by Rosemary and Sigurd, who had the technical specifications reliably at his fingertips. The Trustees expressed themselves impressed and delighted and eventually in need of tea.

A single misfortune had occurred during the months of basic work. Stavros had from the first been absolutely riveted by the lofty, yellow, on-site crane that had been brought in for heavy-duty lifting. That particular morning he was in the cab with Stan Fletcher, the crane driver, who was showing him in detail how the delicate power controls worked. A lengthy steel girder was being moved from a pile onto the developing frame of the building when it unaccountably swung out of control and neatly decapitated a large sculpture that had been temporarily stored there, wrapped against the rain, prior to its relocation to some undecided spot within the new building. Stanley was distraught; it could mean loss of licence for him as he had absolutely no business giving crane lessons to amateur friends on the job. To compound matters the girder had swung back, post decapitation, and dropped bodily onto the remaining torso, crushing it through right down to the feet, and coming to rest on what ended up as a mere pile of twisted bronze. The head, meanwhile, rolled free and came to rest in the mud, its features intact and perfect. The site contractor offered to pay an absolutely whacking sum in compensation provided that no official fuss was made, and Dr Patience confirmed his gentlemanly nature in falling in with this proposal, considerately masking his distress at what had happened. Photographs were quietly taken from all angles to record the details, acting on a reiterated remark from Sigurd as to the benefits of just making sure. Stavros, in due course, made a tidy bit on the scrap metal.

Dr Patience had naturally spared the Trustees the full details of this history as he introduced them to the head of the eponymous captain. A beautifully finished aquarium-like construction had been set flush into the wall near the entrance to the new building. This was large enough to house the head on a graceful base developed by Stavros and Walter to disguise the guillotine work at the neck. When illumined a discreet light set in the ceiling of this promised alcove bestowed on the Captain the most monstrous leer, so that the whole, although respectfully labelled in acknowledgment of the famous bequest, resembled a giant specimen jar in a cosmic gallery of malformed giant foetuses.

Storage, therefore, Dr Patience could write some months later, summing up his *Annual Trustees Report*, for years a nightmare, was now no longer a problem. He was happy to report that all systems were working; the funding would still cover the acquisition of an electronic network, existing staff had happily swapped rooms where they wanted. Everything was unpacked. On top of that, since they had the space, they were even now looking out for one or two new staff members to 'join ship' on this new, triumphant leg of their voyage, under a good head of sail with Captain Samuel Stevenson.

26

A new and go-ahead young Librarian, Mr Stockwell, was the first to be recruited. He was apparently the grand-nephew of someone outside known to Miss Ogilvie, and had submitted an impressive curriculum vitae, the implications of which Montague could only partly comprehend. Young Stockwell was given a small new room with extra plugs, and charged with the responsibility for developing the computer side of things, reporting when necessary directly to the Principal's Secretary. The latter next cozened Montague into coming up with his most choice prose to represent the Last Resort Library electronically to the world. The responsibility weighed heavily on the Principal. This young whippersnapper Stockwell was actually laying down the law about the number of *lines* of text he was permitted, and Dr Patience found that all the fluent expositions and philosophical presentations that he had given over the years now failed entirely to come to his aid. Scribbled and corrected drafts littered his desk like that of any other Unsuccessful Writer, and all this just when he had finally sent his finished *Booklet* off to the printer.

It occurred to Miss Ogilvie while this project was in its infancy to check on what might have already been put out as publicity by the California library. It was a fiddly matter to locate where they had hidden the account of their own reject-collecting practice:

> *Unique in the world, this library also devotes concern to manuscripts of a very different kind. All readers value the rare and famous among manuscripts, and wonder at the creative processes of the great writers captured as they took place, preserved in the ink, with corrections and alterations still there for us to witness in the first versions of our much-loved texts. But in this corner we stop to consider their humbler equivalents, modest,*

lesser writers whose homely, rough-hewn strivings after literature we see also as valid human voices. We offer part of our great library to these modest unsuccessful pen-men and pen-women; we think them important too; and we guard their output with the same dedication and standards as we do our Shakespeare tailor's bill, or all our draft presidential speeches. No other library has undertaken such a task, and we tread this lonely path as pioneers, our concern for unborn readers and sociologists.

Dr Patience's telephone rang just as Miss Ogilvie came in, incredulously holding a print-out of what she had just read. He held up his hand for silence. The operator was explaining that he had a person to person call from the States.

'Hi there, Montague? Great to hear you. I'm Mort G. Zort. Yeah. We are an upcoming new California-based independent television documentary company, Ultra-Big-Lens or UBL, and we'd like to come over and do your library.'

'Evidently you have become confused as to our nature and purpose. We are not a type of dance, or something on a tourist trail.'

He motioned to Miss Ogilvie to pick up the extension receiver at once.

'Hardly confused, Dr.' Mort chuckled. 'It's a long story, I guess. UBL are halfway through a series called *Whatever becomes of...* Sometimes it's one of them child actors, sometimes a fashion that disappears, whatever, – you know the kind of thing. Well, it turns out that the wife of one of our directors was at college with the Director of the American Library here that is your counterpart, so to speak, you know? Well, we decided to do a story about those guys and they told us about how they collect dud manuscripts and that you collect dud manuscripts too and that we thought this would make great television because normal people would think what you guys are doing is a big waste of time sort of thing. Anyway there was some dinner party some place and everybody gets excited you know how they do and one thing leads to another and someone makes a phone call and next thing I'm supposed to do a compare and contrast type thing with them and you guys and make it sound interesting all on a shoestring and tomorrow already. I figure it'd be a great episode. You know, you talking, few close ups, load of crap books, stuff like that. The English side of the story. Mary thought you had some Winston Churchill papers or something?'

'*Episode?*'

'I thought we'd send a good English team to handle things your side. Someone well-known. No point our coming over for just a small thing. They do the shoot, and we put the whole thing together in the can over here in the studio. We can make you guys and our guys even have a conversation or an argument if you want with our new technology. So if it's alright with you we'll ask Mervyn and the team to get in touch. Maybe they could come over early next week, say Monday, Tuesday? It'll be minimal disturbance, I can promise you. One hand-held camera. One mike. Coupla lights. They're in and they're out and you're famous already.'

'Next ....Tuesday....?' Dr Patience looked in bewilderment at his Secretary. She nodded encouragingly and gave him the thumbs up.

'*Do it!*' she whispered.

'Well, I....'

'Great, great. I'll get Merv to call. Speak later, Mont.'

He rang off.

'Rosemary, I think a nervous breakdown might be in order. I am not running this job, it is running me. Should I have it now or later?'

'I think later, Montague. Can I call in Dr Sorensen? This requires discussion.'

'Do, by all means. I'll see what he thinks about my nervous breakdown.'

'Meanwhile, read this.'

She handed him the print-out and left the room. When they returned together the Principal Librarian was statuesque, hands behind his back, looking out through his French windows. He turned, his face grave and determined.

'Sigurd, read this.'

Sigurd did so.

'Rosemary, explain what has just happened.'

Her account was exact and concise.

'Montague, let me get this absolutely straight. This television team has been sicked onto us by Mary-Beth Schumacher's library, who have also put this indefensible and patronising statement out for the world? And they are coming here to interview us next week? Back to back with the Californians?'

'Precisely.'

'You interest me strangely, Principal. I think I see our path clearly here. You too, Rosemary?'

'I seem to remember a yearning for vengeance being expressed in this room in this connection,' said Rosemary mischievously.

'Precisely my point. Okay, when this Mervyn calls, fix it up definitely for Tuesday. I think we can have *everything in place* by the time they arrive.'

'Thank you, Sigurd, sincerely. I appreciate it, the two of you. Perhaps they won't want to speak to me personally at all.'

'Nonsense, Montague. The man at the helm. The Vision, the Voice of Authority. Of *course* they will. Now, Rosemary, let's get a few procedural ideas down on paper with Hugo...'

27

'Well,' said the Television Personality, 'I'm standing in the Central Reading Room of what must be one of the strangest libraries in –'

There was a sudden high-pitched and strident whine.

'My *God*, do you absolutely *have* to hoover in here right now? This is *television* in action. Tel-e-vision? The term familiar to you?'

'Sor-ree!'

The voice was that of Mr Brecknock, who had been taken off cleaning duty months ago, but still remembered how to do it.

'Well,' said the Television Personality, 'I'm standing in the Central Reading Room of what must be one of the strangest libraries in the world. One of the strange things is that there is hardly any light in here, so reading is not as easy as you might think. But I suppose that in some funny way that is quite appropriate –

– somebody find that porter fellow; he seems to know his way around the building, but like all these people he's never around when you need him –

– quite appropriate when you realise that none of these books has ever been published. On the contrary, the unifying factor that has brought them all together under one roof is that very point ...'

The technician spotted Stavros and whispered to him urgently.

'Oh, there you are, Stevie. Can't we do something about this awful blackness? It's going to make terrible television.'

'Is it? I just can't understand what's wrong, Sebastian. Normally our winter arrangements mean it's bright like a summer's afternoon in here. These floor lights are just fire security things, not meant to be proper lights at all.'

Someone trudged through dragging heavy cables, although

it was hard to see who it was. The Television Personality pressed on.

'And here we have one of the custodians of this strange treasure, in Dr Sigurd Sorensen, a man who must have travelled from the far north to take up his post here as Deputy Director?'

'Not to be picky, I was born in Newport Pagnell, and I am in fact *Deputy Principal Librarian* here. My work involves a wide range of duties, varying from administration of the most mundane kind, such as being ultimately responsible for the supply of light bulbs – ironic, in a way, given our wholly unexpected trouble with the lighting system today, usually, I might add, a pleasingly trouble-free system – to advising my boss, the *Principal Librarian* himself, on matters of a far-ranging variety of types. I could probably think of one or two telling examples, deliberately adduced to reflect some idea of the breadth in range of matters that we can need to be discussing, either formally or, of course, informally, depending on the level of sensitivity that seems appropriate...'

'Moving on, perhaps, we - ...'

'I accomplish a lot of this sort of thing, naturally, through statistics, utilising graph paper and graphs, of course, and flow-charts to chart the ... flow ... Flow is *desperately* important. In a way, indispensable. Let me give you a for-instance ...'

Sigurd observed with pleasure that his interviewer was actually moving away from him while he was still speaking. Regretting only that more of the fluent responses up his sleeve were not going to be needed, he disappeared into the gloom to report to the Principal on the Porter's walkie-talkie.

As if by arrangement, Hugo de Butler appeared and smiled warmly. He was, very sensibly, carrying a small torch and held out his card.

'Another side of the library's work is covered by Mr ... de Butler here, who is in charge of assessions.'

'Ah, actually, *accessions*, not "assessions." I am Dr Patience's

Registrar, a funny, rather old-fashioned sounding word that most people usually only hear when they get married, or admit responsibility on paper for their babies, or die. Except that in the latter case, of course, they don't hear it themselves. It means in this context, of course, where life and death interplay is relatively infrequent, that I am officially in charge of all accessions to the Library.'

'Yes, I see. You enjoy that, do you?'

'I do. I have always felt that facilitating modes of access is one of the most important aspects of modern civilised living. It essentially boils down to a reciprocal working relationship; a development of that primary symbiosis which meant that man's crawling out of the slime became possible. I grant access to you: you grant access to me.'

'I simply never thought of it that way.'

'No?'

'Er, thank you.'

The interviewer sat down suddenly on a nearby chair, and could be heard unscrewing the top of what was evidently a metal hip flask. From a distance Stavros watched him wandering fruitlessly around, kicking things in his way. Time for some more help, he thought, concernedly.

'Er, Mr Mervyn, can I introduce you to one of our very best librarians? This is the Honourable Pomfret Payle, who is in charge of Poetry. Would you like to speak to him?'

'Delighted. *Thanks*, Steve. Camera! Well, we turn now to another specialist, a scholar in the best tradition of the word, not a man hemmed up in an ivory tower of his own making, but one able to go out there and make an impact in his chosen field. This is Pommy Pale, who is in charge of poetry in this curious old library. Mr Pale, now *poetry*: that must be a challenging job on a pretty much round the clock basis, I suppose?'

Mr Payle turned slowly, and spoke in very quiet, measured and yet vague tones.

'Well ... sometimes more than others?'

'Interesting, interesting. What's the most unexpected thing that's come in over the last year?'

'Well, most things are expected, actually. There has usually been an exchange of correspondence prior to our formal acceptance. So, we do know they are coming. A word with our Registrar, perhaps, for the details?'

'I see. But in terms of the poetry, I mean, well, we all write poetry at home, don't we; what here on all your shelves has really made you sit up?'

'Mmm ... well... I suppose it depends on what you imply by the question?'

'I was just thinking, like most of our viewers will, I suppose, that probably among all the privately-written poetry that never gets to see the light of day you must come upon the odd unsung genius, the odd overlooked masterpiece?'

My Payle gave this a lot of thought.

'Mmm ... up to a point, I suppose ... depending of course on what you *mean* by genius ... and of course *masterpiece ...*'

He drifted off, distracted by something intangible.

'Well, I guess poetry is often elusive and complex. Let us move over to novels, and ask Mr Grubb, here, who has been Novels Librarian in this library for many years, whether it is true what they say that every man has a book in him, and, if so, is it always a novel?'

'There's more than one place you can keep a novel, I always say.'

'But a majority of amateur writers, if they are to write at all, produce a novel, do they not?'

'Are you speaking statistically or theoretically?'

'Let's have a bash at theoretically.'

'Okay. Go ahead.'

'... Oh, don't I see Mr Richardson over there? Dr Sorensen particularly recommended that I have a word with him. Catch you later...?'

'Certainly. It's been valuable for me, interacting with you, conceptualising my work from the outside, as it were.'

'Mr Richardson? Yes, hi! Now, Mr Richardson, your task is to cover all the unpublished books that do not belong in the other divisions, is that correct?'

'That would be an approximate summary, although possibly slightly weighted in nuance. Not, you see, that my labour is in any way peripheral or secondary, or subsidiary to the more significant needs, aims and achievements of what might be conceived to be more significant aspects of the library's work.'

'No, no, absolutely. I can see that your responsibilities must be extremely taxing. You are clearly in every way the man for the job.'

'Oh, I wouldn't say that. I wouldn't care to say that at all. I applied for Novels, you see. Wanted to move across. More my real field, really, pure unpublished literature. I came ... *third*. So I had to stay with Everything-Else.'

'Well I think you're a lucky man,' said the Television Personality, desperately. 'Let's just have a look at some of the things under your care, at random, as it were ... right on the nearest shelf. What's *this*, for example?'

'Oh, that's something that was passed on to us by the MOD; it had been optimistically submitted to them as a possible Official Publication by a retired quartermaster.'

'What's it called?'

'*How-to-Buy-Contraceptives-in-all-the-World's-Languages.*'

'Uh-huh ... tell me, Mr Richardson, are there any subjects that you would expect to find coming in that somehow ... don't?'

'Yes. Yes there is. *Cricket*. We don't have a single book on cricket. I suppose that no-one has ever been able to come up with a manuscript on cricket that absolutely no-one would publish.'

The Television Personality gesticulated irritably to his cameraman to follow him outside. They were sitting disconsolately on the bench, smoking in silence, when Mervyn suddenly jumped to his feet.

'Well, just as we were about to conclude the day's filming, we fortunately spotted the Principal Librarian himself, in the car park, and were just in time to catch him for a few rounding-up words.'

They ran frantically across the gravel.

'Ah, Principal, just a quick word...?'

'What? Er ... who? Oh, *hel-lo*. The television man. Splendid. How have you got on today? I do hope everyone was helpful. I instructed my staff to do all they could to be of assistance to you and your people in every way. I knew you wouldn't be content with superficial answers. You know, I don't suppose you will necessarily see it in this light, but a film documentary is a multifaceted piece of work. There it is for you, feeding your public, boosting your ratings, paying the mortgage, so to speak, but there is also the other side of the coin: we, thereby, honest toilers in fields, can reach a broader, richer public.'

'Yes, well, exac- '

'Because I just know that there are many, many people out there, writers and authors, story-tellers and poets, working in isolation, following their respective muses, without the comfort of knowing that far ahead there is light at the end of the tunnel. No-one need ever again draw up a will that stipulates "burn all my manuscripts."'

'My company –'

'Because we *want* those manuscripts, you see. We will take those manuscripts. And we will look after those manuscripts. Be they neatly typed, faintly mimeographed, scrawled in pencil, or printed in lipstick capitals, we want them all. For readers yet unborn, we will hold those papers in trust. Those seeds, hand-nurtured and watered, will come in time, against all odds, to bear their fruit. Because, Mr Television, we here *believe* –'

Mervyn spoke tersely, over his shoulder.

'Okay. That's *it*. Sebastian, pack up the camera. Don't forget the first canister. I'm out of here. Where's the van? Jesus, I need a *drink*.'

'…in our work. We have a job to do, yes, but somehow it's more than a job. We deal here, literally, with the humanities. With a capital "H." And there is suffering embodied in those papers. Human suffering, blood … tears and – damn, what was it? – visible right there on the page.'

'Could I have my microphone?'

'Which brings me to my main point, and let me say at this stage how glad I am to have this opportunity of speaking to you all here today. Because we in this Library stand firm to protect the defenceless. We defend those who give birth to their heartfelt words from the *Anti-writers*. The merciless and the heartless. Those in plush offices who *read* and *reject*. Those faceless ones who *skim* and *scorn*, who *riffle* and *return*. The "readers" and the "reviewers," fingers firm on the pulse of commerce, who sport their blinkers and teach what will sell. From these must we protect our people, our nation of unsung wordsmen –'

Mervyn spoke very loudly.

'And so you see us leaving this very extraordinary institution, nestling in the broad bosom of the English countryside, an institution fired by a vision …'

'We hear, you know, from creative, gifted people who have just *given up*. Novelists and poets galore, worn down by brutal rejection and dismissal. I could tell you of cases –'

'*Could I please have my microphone?*'

'Just one of those arrogant rejection letters can shatter a life, ruin a marriage and, worse, still, extinguish completely that subtle fire which burns within the heart of the truly creative –'

The cameraman stepped forward.

'Sod the microphone, Merv. We've got loads. Leave it.'

They walked off across the path, and soon a maroon-painted van was seen to swerve dangerously past the gate house and roar away up the driveway.

Miss Ogilvie stepped out from behind the wall.

'It's okay, Montague. They've gone. All of them. We're safe now. You can sit down. Here, drink this.'

Dr Patience swung round. There stood his trusted Secretary, and Sigurd, Hugo, Ffolke, Pomfret, George and several others, even the excellent Stavros, clutching his receiver. Most of the others, in fact.

'Wonderful, Principal. You were wonderful. We didn't know you had it in you. We were all here listening. Nearly the whole staff. Clear as a bell, you were. Damn it man, we are all proud of you. Half the women were in tears. The whole manifesto can go straight onto the website.'

The Principal Librarian felt close to tears himself. What a team; what a group of supportive, idealistic companions he had!

'*Thank* you, all of you ... I ... I ... It was a great piece of work back there, impeccable planning and faultless execution. Look, let me present this piece of apparatus to Archives.'

Stavros stepped forward to accept it officially.

'You know,' he said confidingly, 'Really stupidly I was going to let the air out of their tyres, but then I realised that it would have exactly the wrong effect. Mind you, we needn't worry about this part of the documentary ever being shown to anyone.'

'How can you be so sure, Stavros?'

'While they were at lunch I opened a couple of can lids and exposed the contents to bright light.'

'Actually, Montague, I think it would be rather a pity if your concluding speech were not syndicated across America on every household TV screen,' said Sigurd, ruefully. 'I should think that the incoming manuscripts would fill the Queen Mary. It would settle the opposition for good.'

The Principal Librarian waved his hand modestly.

'Possibly, Sigurd, possibly, but what is done is done. Stavros acted for the best. We must not kick against fate.'

'I can tell you one thing, Principal,' said Stavros, 'old Merv and the boys won't be coming back *here* for a holiday.'

The Principal Librarian smiled contentedly at his Porter and his Secretary and indeed all his loyal, trusted people.

'You think we really *showed* them, then, what we mean in this Library by the expression *Last Resort?*'

Permanent salaried staff at the time of writing

Principal Librarian:	Dr Dr Cloudesly Montague Patience
Principal Librarian's Secretary:	Miss Rosemary Ogilvie MA DSO
Deputy Principal Librarian:	Mr Sigurd Sorensen
Deputy Principal Librarian's Secretary:	~~Violet Taverner~~ (post vacant)
Registrar:	Mr Hugo de Butler MA
Head of Binding:	Mr McTavish Bristow OBE
Binder's Assistant I:	James Winter
Binder's Assistant II:	Richard Hutton
Head of Conservation & Research:	Dr Harvey Howard Scranton
Assistant, Conservation & Research I:	Miss Elspeth Winterhalter MSc
Assistant, Conservation & Research II:	(post vacant)
Poetry Librarian:	The Hon. Pomfret Payle, MA
Poetry Assistant Librarian:	Louis Brecknock PhD
Drama Librarian:	P. B. Mitcheson
Adult Fiction Librarian:	George G. Grubb
Adult Fiction Assistant Librarian:	Melanie Zong DPhil
Children's Fiction Librarian:	P. Constable-Barber MA
Children's Fiction Assistant Librarian:	Amanda Bickerstaffe BA
Biography & Autobiography Librarian:	Mr Ffolke Leguid
Non-Fiction Librarian:	Oswald Keswick Richardson
Music Librarian (part time):	Guenther Norlund Boehm MA, PhD
Librarians' Secretary:	Wendy Twirl
Librarians' Assistant Secretary:	Rachel Cousens BA
Porter:	Stavros (Steve) Bligh
Porter's Wife:	Millie Bligh
Cleaners:	~~Mrs Woodleigh, Pat Marston~~ (posts vacant)
Groundsman:	Henry Flatman
Groundsman's Assistant:	Willie Flatman (nephew of above)
Canteen Staff:	Sadie Hodge and Prue Florentine
Technician:	Walter Denham

Illustrations

Printed in the United Kingdom
by Lightning Source UK Ltd.
119378UK00004B/61-234